Hex of the Witch

Heather G. Harris

Content Warnings

Please see the full content warnings on Heather's website if you are concerned about triggers.

Please note that all of Heather's works are written in British English with British phrases, spellings and grammar being utilised throughout. If you think you have found a typo, please do let Heather know directly at heathergharrisauthor@gmail.com thank you.

For my awesome supporters on Patreon, with special mention to Amanda Peterman, and Melissa. I am so grateful and humbled by your belief in me.
For Beba – you are an absolute gem and I am so pleased to have you in my life. A million thanks for all you do.

Chapter 1

The building was on fire. Again. I pinched the bridge of my nose and turned to one of the witches who was standing next to me and wringing her hands. 'Tell me you didn't forget to cover your crystal ball.'

Sarah's lip wobbled. 'I'm so sorry, Coven Mother.'

I kept my face carefully neutral, trying to bank my frustration. 'Until you can learn proper potion and crystal-ball care, I'm demoting you to acolyte.' I resisted the urge to apologise but this wasn't Sarah's first mistake, not by a long shot. And her mistakes were *costly*. She needed supervision and her bruised ego would just have to take the hit.

Sarah wailed at my judgement and collapsed sobbing into the arms of her waiting friends. Ria sent me her best death glare, which I blithely ignored. I contemplated giving Sarah a sympathetic little pat on the arm, but I'd just relegated her back to the ranks of a lowly acolyte so

I doubted any comforting gestures from me would be welcome.

I turned back to the newly refurbished building and grimaced at the flames licking at the freshly painted walls.

I hauled out my phone and speed-dialled Dick Symes: Dick by name, dick by nature. Still, the water elemental was local, and one of his extended family would be able to get here faster than the emergency services. No doubt the location of the training house so close to one of the most prestigious water elemental families in the UK was not a simple coincidence but a matter of design by some clever former Coven Mother. Goddess knows, we had needed the elementals often enough lately. The thought made me narrow my eyes again at Sarah.

The phone continued to ring and I struggled to push down my impatience. I didn't need a water elemental in ten minutes, I needed one *now*. Luckily Dick chose that moment to answer. 'Amber DeLea, what do you need?' he asked brusquely.

I appreciated that he got straight to the point. We weren't friends and we didn't need to discuss the weather. 'I need someone to put out a fire at the coven's training house.'

There was a beat of silence. 'Again?'

I couldn't suppress the sigh that slipped out. 'Yes.'

He snickered: *dick*. 'Martin will be with you shortly. It'll cost more this time,' he warned.

I expected nothing less. Nothing is free in the Other realm. 'What do you want?' I asked suspiciously.

'A favour,' he suggested lightly, like it was no big deal.

I wasn't born yesterday. No way was I agreeing to that; it was far too open-ended. 'One favour, to be called in within three months' time. No injury, harm or death to befall anyone as a direct consequence of that favour,' I counter-offered.

'Done,' he agreed triumphantly.

'So mote it be,' I muttered. He sounded entirely too happy for my liking and I hated feeling like I'd got the bad end of a deal.

Dick hung up without another word, and Martin Symes arrived moments later, panting. He'd clearly run from his house – the Symes were *very* local. 'Where do you want me, Miss DeLea?' he asked between pants.

I gestured to the fire behind me, managing to suppress the snarky comment that wanted to slip out. I deserved a medal for my self-control.

'Right you are!' He strode towards the house and seconds later water was pouring from his fingers into the training house. I winced at the damage the torrent was causing, but it put out the fire and that had been the more immediate problem.

'Thank you, Martin. Now can you remove the excess water from the scene?' That was one of the main advantages to using a water elemental instead of the fire department: Martin could soak up all the excess water like a dry sponge. It helped minimise the water damage on top of the fire damage.

He nodded enthusiastically and struck a suitably dashing pose whilst he drew the water back into himself. It would have looked more dashing if he hadn't kept looking over his shoulder to make sure the gaggle of young witches were still watching him.

I called Jeb, the witch who was responsible for coven maintenance. 'Coven Mother, how can I help?' he answered warmly.

'There's been another fire at the training house,' I said, trying to keep my voice even.

'No!' he protested. 'The refurbishment was finished literally yesterday,' he whined, his tone disbelieving.

'Believe me, I know.' Jeb may have organised the work but I'd paid for it. 'You'll need to get to the site to assess the damage.'

'Who was it this time?'

'Sarah Bellington.'

'Again?'

'Indeed. She's been demoted to acolyte.'

He whistled. 'Rightly so, but Venice is going to be so pissed off.' Sarah's mum was a force to be reckoned with – but so am I.

'Goodness that was close. I almost gave a damn,' I snarked back. 'Sarah left her crystal ball uncovered.'

'Oh for fuck's sake,' Jeb cursed loudly. I didn't swear aloud but I wholeheartedly agreed with the sentiment. He cleared his throat. 'Whilst we're sharing bad news, the Crone has returned.'

I frowned. 'What do you mean, she's returned?' The Triune – the Maiden, the Mother and the Crone – had only left that morning after visiting us for three long weeks. Three weeks of seeing to their every need. I'm not used to bowing and scraping – it's not in my skillset – but the Holy Triune demand my respect and, to a degree, my subservience.

It was galling. Of course, I love the Crone herself – Aunt Abigay is one of my mum's best friends and she had helped raise me after my father abandoned us – but our relationship has changed over the years. As the Crone, she holds a sacred, lifelong position in witch society. The Crone is considered to have one of the highest positions in the coven; a position that doesn't allow much room for favouritism or nepotism, more's the pity.

The Triune had left our tower this morning and were supposed to be returning to the coven council in Edinburgh. 'She's back,' Jeb reiterated. 'She requests an audience with you at your earliest convenience.'

'Tell her I'm on my way. You'll have to deal with the situation here.'

'I'm on it, Coven Mother,' Jeb promised.

We hung up and I strode to my waiting car. As I slid into the back seat, I met Oscar's blue eyes in the rear-view mirror. 'Back to the coven, please,' I instructed. I didn't look back at the desolate scene behind me, weeks of work all gone up in smoke because of one idiot's thoughtlessness. Covering your crystal ball is Basic Witchery 101. Sarah was making me look bad and I couldn't afford that – not now.

I wanted to be the witch member for the Symposium. The Symposium runs the Connection, the governing body for all supernatural beings that exist in the Other Realm. There had been a power vacuum ever since Sky, the last witch Symposium member, had been killed.

The coven council was moving excruciatingly slowly in appointing the new member. In the meantime, its members took turns attending the Symposium meetings.

I suspected that they all liked the extra taste of power and weren't in a hurry to relinquish it.

I wanted to be on the Symposium – heck, I wanted to rule it – but one thing at a time. I wanted to craft the change that the Connection so desperately needed, and I wanted to do it from within. Sarah's little stunt made me look bad; if I couldn't handle my own coven, how could I be responsible for all the covens in the country? But the fire had only just happened, so that couldn't possibly be what the Crone wanted with me, could it?

My driver sensed my foul mood so he didn't try for chitchat. Oscar is more than a driver and bodyguard to me – he's been my mother's partner for many years. They'd never formalised their union and now, with Mum's dementia, the opportunity had passed. But Oscar is the father I'd never had after mine skipped out on Mum and me when I was six years old. I was glad she had found happiness in Oscar's arms and only a smidgen jealous that such love had been denied to me.

We pulled up to the coven tower. In the old days, covens lived together in villages but we have modernised our living practices to adapt to modern life and now the covens own their apartment blocks. At the top of mine is a rarely used guest suite that The Crone had been occupying for the last few weeks. No doubt she'd be waiting for me there.

I took the stairs. At forty-two years of age, I need to make the effort to incorporate exercise into my day or the pounds will pile on – especially as I have a weakness for blueberry muffins. When I reached the guest suite, I knocked once on the door.

'Come in,' the Crone called.

She was sitting in a high wingback chair, white afro resting languidly against the purple fabric. She sat up as I walked in and met my eyes. Her dark skin bore a few lines of age but not as many as she was due.

I knew I was in trouble because her pink lipstick-painted lips didn't curve into a smile and her eyes were cold. 'Aunt Abigay—' I started.

She looked at me with a hint of censure. I wasn't her family to be gifted her name now that she was the Crone. 'Coven Mother,' she responded sharply. 'You've been keeping secrets.'

Chapter 2

I said nothing. When in doubt, silence is golden.

She arched an elegant eyebrow. 'Do you have so many secrets, child, that you do not know to which one I am referring?'

Yup. 'Enlighten me,' I suggested.

'You've been working on a potion to extend our time in the Other realm.' Ah. *That* secret.

There are two main realms: the magical one that is called the Other realm, and the non-magical one known as the Common realm. They exist together, running concurrently.

I explain the realms to new witches by asking them to imagine that they are short-sighted. When you are in the Common you have no glasses and you are blind to the magical dangers around you. Step into the portal and out into the Other realm and it is like putting on the correct pair of glasses; suddenly you can see everything around you – fire elementals, dragons, ogres. Everything magical is revealed to you and, of course, you have full access to your own magic. Glasses or not, the magic is always there; it is just a question of whether you can see it and utilise it.

As with everything, there is a catch. If you are on the human side of the Other realm like witches, wizards, werewolves, elementals and vampyrs, then once you are introduced to the Other you must continually hop back and forth between the realms. We humans have to charge our magical batteries in the ordinary world (the Common realm) ready for use in the magical world (the Other realm). It's annoying and inconvenient, not to mention dangerous.

The creatures – dragons, dryads, ogres, satyrs and centaurs – don't have the same restriction. They have an advantage in that they don't need to go to the Common realm and they can exist wholly in the Other if they want to. They never have to be without their magic. I had long since decided that it is this disparity that lies at the heart of all human–creature tensions.

A human faction had been spouting Anti-Creature rhetoric. They imaginatively called themselves the Anti-Crea and they wanted a world where the creatures were tagged and monitored like animals.

Of late, there had been increasing tension between the two groups, which then escalated into violence and a full-blown battle. The Anti-Crea had not come out well from a fight with the dragons and their human counterparts, the brethren. The brethren were raised to be as deadly as Rambo, so the battle had reached its inevitable conclusion. For now the Anti-Crea were licking their wounds but the situation couldn't continue. If I could develop a potion that significantly extended the time the human side could spend in the Other, maybe I could reduce that tension. I wasn't naïve enough to think it would resolve *everything* – but it would be a damned good place to start.

'It's not that much of a secret,' I defended myself. I was stretching the truth a little because I hadn't told another soul about my potion research. I hadn't wanted to put it out there and then have it fail.

My time was limited, though. Eventually, after making agonisingly slow progress during the last six months, I'd had to give in and apply to the council for help. 'I got an initial grant, and I made an application to the coven council for a temporary Coven Mother to take over whilst I focus on the potion,' I told the Crone.

Being a Coven Mother is a coveted position. I didn't want to step aside from it, but I was struggling to juggle all my duties and work on the potion. The latter had to be my priority because it had the potential to be life changing. With this potion, I could achieve something huge for the Other Realm.

With a temporary Coven Mother here, I honestly believed that I could make the potion in less than a week. That would give me time to source and harvest the final ingredients and make the final brew; I already had a base ready in stasis.

'Yes,' the Crone harrumphed. 'That application is why I'm here. The coven council is concerned that you have painted a target on your back. They fear that news of your project will leak and that the creatures will seek to kill you to put an end to your research.'

I blinked. 'I haven't told a soul about my application or my project, so I don't see how it will leak.'

'Evidently it already has,' the Crone said grimly. 'Your application appears to have been ... misplaced.'

'My application marked "highly confidential, for the coven council's eyes only"?' I asked drily.

'Yes. That one. The council believe that they have now...' she paused '...stemmed the leak, but further steps are needed to ensure your safety. To that end, they have hired the griffins to protect you.'

Horror flooded through me. 'No! You know how I feel about them!' A griffin had killed the love of my life, Jake.

The griffins are on the creature side of the Other realm. They have no need to go to the Common realm or experience life without their power if they don't want to. Instead, they have their own cross to bear: they have to battle a constant compulsion to kill.

When the Connection came to power some eighty years ago, they hired the griffins to carry out their black ops; they also gave them permission to open their own assassins' guild. The Connection wanted them to channel their deathly urges into more ... productive pursuits. Consequently, all kills carried out by the griffins nowadays are sanctioned by the guild or the government.

All too often history has shown us that if a griffin does not kill within a certain time frame, their lethal urges can take over and a deadly massacre will follow. Since the guilds' inception, there have been no more accidental slaughters. Evidently, the guild has its own rules as to what makes a target acceptable or not.

For some reason, Jake had ticked all the boxes.

'I am aware of your issues, princess.' Aunt Abigay's tone softened and I was pleased I'd been promoted from child to princess, the term of endearment from my youth. She continued. 'Regardless, hiring them is the only way to guarantee your safety. If the griffins are hired to *protect* you, it creates a conflict of interest such that they are unable to accept a contract to *kill* you.'

I could see the wisdom of that because the guild has never failed to carry out a contract. The ogres are hit or miss; they are paid on a 'time-spent' basis. If they don't manage to kill the target in the given time frame then you pay more or the target walks away. It is different with the griffins; if they accept a hit on you, you die. Always.

'Okay,' I admitted reluctantly. 'I guess that makes sense, but I think the council is over-dramatizing. No one is going to want to kill me.'

'If you think that then you're being naïve, Amber,' the Crone said bluntly. 'But that's not the bad news.'

I stilled. What could be worse that having a griffin bodyguard? 'If that's not the bad news, then what is?'

She looked at me with far too much sympathy. I wasn't going to like what was about to come out of her mouth. 'The griffin that has been hired to protect you is Bastion.'

'No! No way. No way in hell!' I spat. Bastion was the griffin who killed Jake. Of all of the creatures in all of the realms, he was the sole being I couldn't stand. 'No,' I repeated.

'The guild was quite clear. It was him or no one.'

'Why? Why him?'

'It is a term of their protection that you must first remove the witch's curse from him,' she said reluctantly.

That was the nail in the coffin. I folded my arms. 'Absolutely not.'

Bastion had once walked into a black witch's trap and the curse was slowly draining his life force. I might not be willing to kill Bastion, but I was prepared to sit back and watch the curse do it for me. He would still die but my hands would be blessedly clean. Maybe that was sophistry, but I found I didn't really care.

'If you do not remove the curse and accept Bastion as your protector, you are as good as dead,' Aunt Abigay said steadily. 'Someone will hire the griffins to kill you – and the ogres, too. The deadliest of the creatures will come for you and your research. You won't last five minutes.'

Ye of little faith. 'I think you're being ridiculous. You're blowing the risk level way out of proportion,' I argued.

'Not just me but the council, too. If you do not accept this safety measure, the council will not allow you to continue your experiment. The risk is too high.' I knew that she wasn't talking about the risk to me but the risk that my research would fall into the wrong hands.

She leaned forward and took my hand. 'Don't you see? This is a test Amber. Can you – *will* you – put the council's needs ahead of your own? Will you do what is right for your people even though it is wrong for you personally?' Abigay squeezed my hand. 'You and I both know that the Goddess has said you are destined for greatness. This is your moment, Amber. Will you really deny yourself your dreams out of spite?'

'I won't work with Bastion,' I said tightly. 'I won't save him.'

She released my hand and leaned back. As her lips pressed in a thin line, her disappointment in me was plain to see and it stung. She reached up and grasped the pendant around her neck, and she sent her eyes skywards, as if she was praying for strength. She let out a soft sigh and returned her eyes to me. 'If you do not agree to having a protector, the coven will deny your application and forbid you to continue with this experiment. We can't afford for such data to fall into the wrong hands simply because you are headstrong. You either make history with Bastion or you sink into obscurity. Alone.'

'Obscurity, then,' I snarled around gritted teeth.

'Then you have failed, and I have failed you.' Abigay released her amulet, moved to the edge of her seat and tried to stand up. I offered her my arm. 'It was so much easier to make a dramatic exit when I was younger,' she muttered, pulling a smile from me.

Once she was standing, she sighed and gently touched my face. 'You know I love you, Amber. As your mother got sicker, I promised her I would look out for you. Do not make me break my oath to her.'

My mother is still with us – but at the same time she isn't. Dementia is a vile illness: she has good days and bad days, but never normal days. Abigay had visited her every single day during her three-week stay, but Mum never recognised her best friend. That hadn't stopped Abigay from going. For some, the blank looks would have been too much to bear but Abigay was happy to pretend to be a new acquaintance if it meant she could be with my mum again.

'I'm not,' I insisted, my throat tight. 'You *are* looking out for me – but you can't make my choices for me.'

'No,' Abigay agreed, suddenly looking all of her eighty years, 'I cannot. I just hope you live long enough to regret them.' She swept out of the room without looking back. Despite what she'd said about her age, she was still pretty good at dramatic exits.

Chapter 3

The door burst open and slammed into the metal cabinet next to it. Chips of wood flew into the room from the impact. 'You'll pay for that,' I snapped, mentally making a note to send the intruder an invoice.

'You're a vindictive bitch,' Bastion snarled at me.

I studied him for a moment as I contemplated my reply. Dark haired with brown eyes and warm, tanned skin, his chiselled jaw was covered with several days' worth of stubble. He was gracing my office in his human form, dressed in his usual black combat trousers and black T-shirt that might as well have been painted on. But for once he looked like crap, far worse than the last time I'd seen him. There were dark shadows under his eyes and exhaustion in every line of his body.

The curse was finally taking its toll and surely even he couldn't survive much longer. Was I a vindictive bitch? Yes. But did he deserve to die? Absolutely. He had killed

Jake, the love of my life, my best friend – and for much of my life my only friend.

'Please find somewhere else to exist,' I instructed him coolly.

He glared at me but didn't respond. Okay then: I needed to be more blunt. I turned back to my paperwork as if he were unimportant. 'Kill me or say your piece and leave, but don't waste my time.' I can't stand time wasters. Mum had taught me that every moment we have on this earth is precious and I didn't want to waste a single one on him.

'You're condemning me to die,' he growled.

Finally I looked up. 'As you have already done to so many others.'

'It's my job.'

'A job is something you do. You are an assassin – death is a part of every breath you take.'

'I'm a griffin.' He said it like it explained everything. Maybe it did, but the man before me was the worst of the worst. Bastion: his name was a like a curse in my mouth. And yes, I was condemning him to death. I'm a lot of things; I'm a witch, a bitch, and yes, I'm petty as heck. But my grudge with Bastion wasn't petty; it was justified. And he'd die for it.

'I know about the deal that Shirdal made with the council,' Bastion snarled. 'My services in exchange for you removing this damned curse. But last night he rang and said the deal is off because you'd refused to work with me.' He glared at me. 'You're killing me.' He bit off the phrase oddly as if he'd stopped himself from saying more.

I didn't care what else he had to say; I cared more about Shirdal. Shirdal is Bastion's boss and head of the griffins' assassin guild. I actually like Shirdal and I have no quarrel with him. He hadn't killed someone I loved.

'I'm doing nothing of the sort,' I said evenly, staring at Bastion. 'The witch's curse is killing you. It has nothing to do with me.'

'Sophistry,' he bit out. 'You could remove the curse if you wanted to. Do you think that you're the only witch I know? I've approached them all but no one will help me because you've blacklisted me. You're killing me just as surely as the black witch,' he growled.

It was the most I'd ever heard the laconic man say, and it infuriated me. How dare he whine about his fate when he had killed so many? 'You killed Jake,' I shouted back.

'HE WANTED TO DIE!' Bastion roared.

The words hit me like a fist to the stomach, and thought and reason fled. My heart hollowed and my eyes filled with tears. 'Get out,' I whispered, hating the wobble in my voice and the hotness in my eyes.

Bastion scrubbed a hand through short black hair. 'Miss DeLea, I'm sorry – I shouldn't have—'

'Leave!' I hissed.

He squared his shoulders and walked out, shutting the damaged door behind him. When I was alone, I let the tears fall. The worst of it was, I knew he was telling the truth.

When we'd dated, Jake was bright and vivacious, the centre of every room and the heart of every party. I had been honoured and amazed that he'd wanted to be with *me,* quiet, awkward me. Was it any wonder that I'd fallen head over heels for him? But then he'd been targeted for assassination. A vile black potion thrown in his face should have killed him but I'd used my family grimoire to save him, faked his death and put him into hiding. He'd remained alive but hidden for twenty years.

But hiding had changed him. Every day he grew a little quieter, a little more bitter about all he had left behind in exchange for staying alive. It was a half-life, and in the end he'd blamed me for it.

Right up until the day that Bastion had killed him.

I couldn't sleep. I'd worked late before collapsing into bed and my eyes were gritty and sore. Exhausted as I was, though, I still tossed and turned. Sleep wouldn't come and I could get no respite from the thoughts that were whirling in my head.

Exhausted but unable to sleep: that was how the witch's curse worked on Bastion. The thought made my conscience prickle uncomfortably. The curse would deny him sleep until his body started to break down. Was the Goddess trying to tell me something? Because if so, I had my fingers in my ears and was singing 'la-la-la' very loudly.

I kicked off the duvet. I needed to consult with the one person I knew who would agree with me. Of course it was the right thing to give up on the potion rather than work with Bastion; I just needed someone to agree with me and tell me that Aunt Abigay was wrong.

I strode over to the wooden cupboard in my bedroom and opened the door to reveal the safe hidden inside it. When I put in the correct combination, the door opened. I gave the stuffed toy cat inside a quick cuddle – it was a childhood gift from Abigay – then I put it back and reverently lifted out the DeLea grimoire.

I laid Grimmy – named by my adolescent self – on my bed then carefully stroked his spine. It wasn't long since we'd last spoken so he awoke easily, levitated off the bed and flipped his pages as he did his equivalent of stretching.

'Why, Miss DeLea! Is it very late or very early that we are meeting in your bedchamber?' His warm Alabama accent made me smile. I'd grown up hearing that Deep South gentleman's drawl whilst Mum had consulted with the grimoire in secret. Many a night I'd sneaked from my bed to peek at them both when I should have been sleeping.

Grimmy had spent a couple of centuries in the Americas with my ancestors. He loved to talk of his time in Alabama, though the less said about his time in Salem the better. He'd been in the UK for more than three hundred years but he clung to his drawl like a barnacle to a whale. Even after all this time, I still had no idea how he projected his voice into the world. Magic, I supposed.

'It's late, Grimmy. Sorry to bother you but I need some advice.'

'Some advice from *me*?' If he'd had eyebrows, I knew that they'd be shooting up. Grimmy is my responsibility now that Mum can't sustain him. It is up to me to make sure he has enough life force to keep going. He is a treasure and an heirloom, and he holds centuries of carefully stored knowledge. He is also a teensy bit forbidden, so he stays hidden from prying eyes.

Now that it's my job to sustain him, I don't usually pull him out for a quick chat. I had done when I was younger; back when I didn't understand what it was costing Mum to sustain him. The thought that her dementia might have been caused in some way by my late-night chats with Grimmy ate me up inside. And was I doomed to suffer the same fate if I kept on consulting him? I didn't think so; none of my ancestors had been similarly afflicted. It was just dementia, a vile but natural disease.

'Advice from you,' I agreed. Grimmy is the product of the era in which he was made, and he has some old-fashioned beliefs. Anti-Crea ones, to be precise. If there was anyone I could rely on to agree with me, it would be Grimmy. 'I've been working on a project,' I confessed. 'A secret one.'

'Why, Miss Amber! Do tell me more.' His voice was eager; Grimmy loves an illicit project. The book took on a soft golden glow, which he does when he's really excited about something.

I cleared my throat. 'I've been studying a lot of potion theory, and I've started to work on one that I believe could extend our time in the Other realm. Extend it significantly.'

'That would be amazing. What a potion! What a purpose! The DeLea name would be remembered for all of time!' Grimmy said excitedly.

'Right. But there's a catch.'

He gave a huffing laugh. 'Isn't there always?' he asked cynically, his enthusiasm cooling. 'Go on. Tell me all about it.'

'The council has decreed that I can only continue to work on the project if I am protected by a griffin.'

'It is good that they take your welfare so seriously.'

I snorted. 'It has nothing to do with my welfare,' I said sceptically. 'They don't want me to die in case my killer steals my research notes. They simply want to make sure my research doesn't fall into the wrong hands.'

'That's understandable. This is a volatile project. It could change the socio-political structure of the Other realm. So what's holding you back?'

I blinked. He seemed to have no problem with me working together with a creature. 'Well, the griffin that the guild has offered is Bastion.'

'The one that killed your Jake?' Grimmy asked.

'Exactly.'

Grimmy had been instrumental in faking Jake's death. He was the only one on this blessed earth that had known about it at the time besides me and Jake. I'd used black runes from Grimmy's pages to heal Jake, to keep him alive, and I wondered at times if they had somehow corrupted him. The black runes had brought Jake back for a miserable half-life that he'd no longer wanted.

'So you work with the griffin,' Grimmy said calmly. 'What other option is there? To deny yourself your destiny? To deny the DeLea name its glory? You *must* make the potion, Miss Amber. To do anything else would be absolute folly!' He closed his pages with a slam, the light faded from the book and he hit the bed hard. The heavy tome rested there, silent and accusing. Grimmy had sent himself back to sleep rather than talk to me. Great, even books didn't want to be my friend.

Rune ruin! I had been banking on Grimmy's support, but if even *he* thought I should work with Bastion then maybe I *did* need my head examined. Maybe he was right. Was it crazy to deny myself my chance for greatness just because of one damned griffin?

Chapter 4

I awoke clear headed and resigned. I wanted to work with Bastion as much as I wanted to shove a burning rod of iron into my eye, but I'd do it. With this potion I could change thousands of lives for the better – even save thousands of lives if it helped cool the conflict between the creatures and the Anti-Crea. And it wouldn't hurt my bid to get that much-coveted position on the Symposium. I'd make the potion, take the exams and then I'd be a shoo-in.

This potion was the key to accomplishing something wonderful, to achieving everything I'd ever wanted, and it would be foolish to throw it all away because I didn't like Bastion. I would save the prick and pray that he'd fall foul of another curse. Or maybe he could die saving me – that would be poetic justice.

I kicked off the duvet and went into the bathroom, where I showered perfunctorily to scrub the sleep from my skin and my brain. After I was clean and dry, I braided my auburn hair to get it out of the way then grabbed my strongest protection potion and painted some runes on my skin, including protection from fire and vampyrs. No matter how good my runes are, I'm still not immune to fire like a dragon but the runes were better than nothing. If a fire elemental flung a fireball at me, I might still have burns but I'd live. Hopefully.

I took the time to paint anti-vampyr runes on my neck, wrists and inner thighs – vampyrs so love a pulse point – then I pulled out my magic and let it run along the rune lines. A firmer tug of my magic made them shine once and then disappear so they were invisible to the naked eye.

Ready to face the day, I sent an abrupt message to summon Bastion and a more polite message to Abigay to tell her that I'd changed my mind and that I would work with Bastion.

I picked up the hand mirror on my bedside table, put it on my lap and looked into my green eyes. For a moment I was lost in memory and I saw Mum in my mind's eye, standing behind me, her hands resting on my shoulders. 'Look at yourself, Amber, and tell yourself how strong you are. What are you going to achieve today? What are you going to do today to make yourself proud?'

No matter how old I was, no matter how far gone she was with dementia, her voice would always be with me, pushing me to achieve the greatness she'd always known I was capable of.

I cleared my throat and started the mantra I'd been repeating virtually every day of my life. As I met my own gaze in the mirror I said firmly, 'I am strong. I don't need a familiar to fit in. I have everything I need within me to succeed. Today my goal is ... to save my enemy.'

Saying it aloud made it real. I was going to save Bastion's life and in return he was going to protect mine. I frowned at the thought. I didn't *need* a griffin protector; I knew what I was doing.

I opened the curtains and stifled a shout of surprise when I saw a familiar raven hovering in front of my living room window. 'Fehu!' I greeted the bird. 'You scared the life out of me.'

I unlocked the balcony door and touched the warding rune to allow him in. Fehu had flown into my life a few weeks earlier. His wings had been cruelly broken, no doubt used in a black witch's ritual that needed pain to fuel it. He'd escaped, though I had no idea how, and crashed onto my balcony. The identity of the black witch remained a mystery, a really sore spot for me. I'd healed the avian and named him Fehu after the rune for good luck. He'd visited me regularly ever since, though I think mostly for the fancy ham that I throw his way.

HEATHER G. HARRIS

Fehu flew straight to my kitchen and landed on the sink taps. I put my hands on my hips and huffed good-naturedly. 'You're wanting ham, then.' I opened the fridge and pulled out a few choice pieces that he snaffled down happily.

Fehu was someone's familiar but not mine. Never mine. I'd been watching the area around the coven for the last few weeks but I hadn't seen so much as a midnight-black feather to suggest that he belonged to someone local. It bothered me that he'd flown to me because he couldn't have travelled far with his wings snapped like that. Whoever the black witch was, I feared that they lived in my tower.

After he'd eaten his fill of the ham, Fehu sat on my shoulder. He nuzzled my ear and gave a soft kraa as I stroked his silky feathers, then he carefully tucked some loose hairs back into my plait. 'Thank you,' I said when he finished grooming me. 'Here, you can have some more ham for that.'

He gave a happy warble and hopped from foot to foot. Once he was fed, he flew to my balcony door and gave a happy trill. Obligingly, I let him out again. 'Don't be a stranger, Fehu.'

He gave a kraa and flew onto the metal railing of the balcony. He was still not leaving and that warmed my heart. 'You keeping an eye on me?' I asked. He tilted his head as if he were listening. 'I'm going down to my coven office now. Ground floor,' I explained.

He bobbed his head, took off and swooped downwards. I wondered if he would indeed be sitting outside my office when I got there. In the coven it is never wise to underestimate the intelligence of animals, many of whom are bonded familiars just like Fehu. The bonding itself doesn't necessarily add extra intelligence but it gives a much-needed communication route, letting the witch and their familiar interact telepathically to a degree.

I had no first-hand experience of that, but my mum had said she could send visions and feelings to Lucille, her ferret familiar. Through those visions she could give Lucille instructions; for example, she could show Lucille an image of a ferret picking up an item in another room and bringing it back. That had amused me for hours as a child as I dreamed of my own familiar bond that never came.

A witch without a familiar: I was an absurdity. I'd tried never to let my lack constrain me, but the other coven kids hadn't been kind.

I left my apartment and went downstairs. I have a home office in my apartment, but I do paperwork in the coven one. Now that the training house had been destroyed – again – I'd also be doing some one-on-one tutorials there.

I looked out of the window and, sure enough, Fehu was sitting in the branches of a nearby tree. I gave him a brief smile and got down to work. I turned on my computer and ran through the logbooks. We had a corporate runing booked for later that day and I made a note to remind Ethan to ensure all the anti-vampyr runes were added on. Commercial properties don't have any inherent protection against vampyrs strolling in, so the runes need to be added for extra protection against them. Ethan knew that already but I struggle not to micromanage – besides, what if I didn't say anything and he forgot? I wouldn't have our coven's reputation in ruins.

There was nothing else major on the books, just some minor cosmetic healing jobs that had been pencilled in. The only other thing was a scrying job: Meredith Plath was scheduled to do a complex scrying later for a very old case of a missing person, and she had requested permission for her daughter, Ria, to observe. Ria had been in the same class as Sarah; fortunately *she* appeared to have actually absorbed some of the rules that we try to instil.

Ria had recently graduated from acolyte to witch, so observing a complex scrying was a good learning opportunity even if the scry was unsuccessful. Meredith is one of my best witches but so far Ria's magic had fallen short of the brilliance of her mother's. Never mind; I had no doubt she would find her place.

I checked the overnight logs and frowned when I saw that we'd had three calls for emergency healing, all from vampyr attacks. That was unusual. These days vampyrs have blood donors and blood bags can be delivered to their door; feeding from sentient beings is a big no-no. The Connection doesn't like it when we eat each other. Besides, magical blood never does quite what you expect it to do; for example, feeding from a wizard would leave a vampyr higher than a kite and more violent than a griffin.

Sure enough, the first victim was a wizard, the second victim was a dryad and the third one a siren. Normally three feeds would be more than enough to leave *any* vampyr sated, but one that had drunk wizard's blood would keep on attacking.

Vampyrs can stroll around in the daylight; the belief in the Common realm that they can't stand sunlight is a complete myth. They aren't nocturnal like fiction says, and they can move in the sun like anyone else; the only risk to them is skin cancer if they don't use sun cream, just like the rest of us. However, they do prefer to hunt in the dark because in darkness they can phase and use shadows to move instantly from one place to another.

Combining that with their incredible speed means that night is a dangerous time for the weak to stroll around – or it had been until the Connection intervened and instituted the 'no eating each other' rule.

Daylight or not, a rogue, wizard-addicted vampyr was on the prowl. When I checked the overnight log again, I saw that Timothy Woodman had been in charge. I clicked my tongue. Timothy was work-shy and always did the bare minimum. I fired off an email setting out the obvious link between the attacks and querying his lack of forethought in contacting the relevant authorities.

After that I hastily typed a second email, in which I anonymised the details of the victims and sent it to the local vampyr clan – their vampyr, their mess. For good measure, I cc'd it to one of the Connection's inspectors whom I knew well. Elvira Garcia wasn't currently local to here but she knew how to pull strings. She'd make sure that the attacking vampyr was dealt with, one way or another.

Chapter 5

I watched Henry as he practised another rune throw and frowned. The acolyte wasn't even holding the rune stones to his heart. 'Your heart, Henry. Why do you keep forgetting to hold the stones to your heart? How can you not know where the most important organ in your body is?'

'Second most important,' the teenager smirked.

Goddess, did he just make a cock joke? I gave him a glare that made his smirk falter. If he wasn't willing to put in the time and effort then I was done with him – for today, at least. 'Henry, your absence is required.'

He blinked. 'What?'

I made a shooing motion. 'Leave!' I like teaching those who are passionate and willing to learn but teaching the various 'Henrys' in the coven is hard work. I can't abide laziness or abject stupidity. If Henry was joking about his cock then he wasn't taking his work seriously and he needed to. If he mucked up rune work someone could die – including him.

Henry gathered his stones and left.

My stomach growled. It was 2pm and lunchtime had been and gone, lost in hours of tutorials and a pile of paperwork. I was impatient for the coven council to appoint someone as a temporary Coven Mother so I could focus on my potion project. I'd already spent an inordinate number of evenings in research and I was itching to build on the theoretical work. I needed some unusual ingredients to get the potion to work and I was desperate to retrieve them and get started.

I decided to pop up to my flat for a quick sandwich then come back down to my coven office for the remaining office hours. It is rare for anyone to take me up on my open-door policy but I believe in making myself accessible. I glanced out at my window as I left and felt a sting of disappointment that Fehu had already gone. He must be a busy raven: places to go, people to see, things to do.

I took the stairs rather than the lift. I have a suite of rooms, spanning the whole second-to-the-top floor of the tower block – there has to be an advantage to being the boss. I have an open-plan lounge, dining room and kitchen, all in one gloriously large and airy space. My bedroom and bathroom are next to the living-room area, and my home office is off the dining area. I expect it's supposed to be a guest bedroom but I don't have enough friends to justify that. Using it as an office space is far more sensible.

I went into the black granite kitchen and made short work of building and eating a sandwich that I washed down with the fresh orange juice Oscar makes for me every day. He's been making it for me since I was in my teens to ensure I get plenty of good vitamins. Twenty years later, and despite the fact that I am perfectly capable of making my own juice, he is still doing it. It makes me smile every morning to see a fresh glass waiting in my fridge; it is evidence that someone still cares for me.

I barely took a fifteen-minute break but that would have to do. Time is money and I needed to earn a lot. Mum's care is paid for in advance – for the whole year – and potion ingredients are pricey. I'd been buying a lot of them and I'd need even more before my potion was finished. I could have applied for another grant, but given that the council had already 'misplaced' my application for a temporary Coven Mother it didn't seem like the best idea. If I wanted to fly under the radar, it would be best not to file any more documents with the council if I could avoid it.

I left my flat and jogged down the stairs back to my coven office. My breath caught as I walked in. Sitting at my desk, in *my* seat, was Bastion. He looked awful, even worse than he had the day before. I ignored the twinge of conscience and glared at him. 'Get out of my seat.'

He rose instantly. 'Don't get your knickers in a twist. I just didn't want to wait with my back to a door.' He gestured to the guest chair opposite my desk.

'Don't think for one second that you have *any* effect on my knickers,' I harrumphed as I reclaimed my chair.

'You changed your mind,' Bastion said carefully. 'Thank you.'

'I'm not doing it for you, not for one second. I am doing it for the potion.' And all the people it could help.

He held up his hands; I suspected it wasn't a gesture he often made. 'Your motivation is your own. When can we break the curse?'

I grimaced. No time like the present, I guessed. If he was going to protect me, it was in my best interests to have him fighting fit as soon as possible. At the moment, he looked like a firm push would send him sprawling. 'Now is fine. Do you have the witch's blood with you?' The only way to undo a curse like this was to use the blood of the witch that had cursed him. Luckily, he'd managed to secure some.

'Yes, it's in a cooler with ice bags. It's still frozen.'

'Fine. Bring it up to my flat.' He knew the way; he'd been there once before when he'd browbeaten me into helping him find a missing griffin. It transpired that the missing griffin was his daughter, Charlize.

Charlize seemed to have a little problem with obeying rules. She'd broken them a time or two and someone had, quite rightfully in my opinion, got pissed at her for killing the wrong person. She'd been kidnapped and I'd had to bend the rules to find her. The pay for that job had been enough to pay for Mum's care fees for the next year, so it had been worth it even though helping Bastion had stuck in my craw. I guess that foreshadowed all that was to come, I thought grumpily. Here I was, once again helping the man I despised above all others. The Greater Good had better appreciate all my hard work.

Bastion left my office to retrieve his cooler from wherever he'd stashed it, and I headed upstairs to prepare my room and my equipment. I relaxed the wards to allow Bastion to come inside and rolled up the circular rug on the lounge floor. Underneath it is a huge white pentagram painted onto the wooden floorboards – I am always ready for a runing. I walked around the pentagram, double-checking for any flakes of paint, but it was perfect.

Next, I disappeared into my wardrobe and pulled out two fluorescent pink and purple hula hoops. Each one was made up of four hollow pieces that slotted together to form a circle. I poured salt carefully into a segment of the pink hoop then attached the next segment before filling that with salt, too. When all four segments were salt-filled and reattached, I started on the purple one. Unlike traditional salt circles that are poured on the floor, catching these with your toe doesn't suddenly break them and expose you to a host of black magic that can invade your body and your soul. Plus, they are mess free *and* reusable.

Despite their clear advantages, the coven council had rejected my repeated requests to roll out the salt hoops to the rest of the UK witches. Apparently they weren't *seemly*, which was a load of hogwash. My coven had started using them years ago, earning us the ridiculous moniker of the 'hula witches'. It made us seem like we were constantly ready for a lūʻau, but who cared? Sticks and stones may break my bones but breaking a salt circle will kill me.

I filled the kettle and set it to boil then opened the sliding doors to the balcony and studied the potted plants. I selected my least favourite one, a hardy, white-flowering shrub that had survived months of neglect. I'm not green-fingered at the best of times and being consumed by my potion project meant little else had received my attention. I quickly watered the other plants, carried the small white one inside and set it down by the pentagram.

I shut all the curtains, not because the magic workings needed darkness but because I disliked the idea of prying eyes watching the proceedings – even though my rooms were on the sixth floor and a Peeping Tom was as likely as a vegetarian griffin.

There was a sharp knock on the door, and I surveyed the room one last time before opening it. Bastion was leaning against the door jamb with the cooler at his feet, as if standing was too much effort. He pushed himself upright, lifted the cooler and walked in. His gait was smooth and he didn't stumble, but I could see the effort he was making.

I watched him dubiously; he couldn't even protect me from so much as a sniffly cold in this state. 'The blood?' I asked.

He pulled out a large bag of frozen blood from the cooler. I relaxed when I saw the size of it; I'd have plenty to work with. I took it to my kitchen counter and poured freshly boiled water into a glass bowl. 'Come and hold the blood bag upright so none of the water leaks in,' I ordered Bastion.

He obeyed, carefully placing the blood bag into the hot water but keeping the seal clear of it. While he held the bag in place, I readied my paintbrushes. I had a decent amount of blood to work with but a lot of runes to paint, so I selected a few of the smallest brushes. Once I started runing I didn't want to stop to clean the brushes of the inevitable clots, so having a good supply was a must. Next I pulled on gloves – only an idiot in this day and age messes about with blood without adequate protection. A host of nasty diseases and bugs can be transmitted in blood and I wasn't taking any chances.

I busied myself with my preparations, which was preferable to speaking to Bastion, until the blood was ready to work with.

Bastion finally spoke into the silence. 'It's ready.'

I nodded and retrieved my wooden bloodworking bowl. Bloodwork isn't inherently black magic any more than a knife is inherently evil; it is how you use it that matters. Today I was using bloodwork to save Bastion's miserable life, so my soul was sparkly clean – in this, at least.

Chapter 6

I painted the last of the defence rune *thurisaz* and stretched my cramping fingers. Five clumpy brushes lay discarded to one side. Runes are intricate, and it had taken over an hour to paint the ones needed to break the witch's curse.

I stood and walked around the pentagram, checking every single rune. One mistake and I wouldn't be breaking the witch's curse, I'd be adding to it. Satisfied, I passed one of the hula hoops to Bastion. He took it dubiously, eyeing it with visible disdain. I couldn't resist a jibe. 'Not manly enough to carry off pink?' I taunted.

He met my eyes. Immediately my every instinct started to scream that he was a predator and that I was going to die. I raised my chin defiantly and held my ground by sheer strength of will, cementing my feet to the floor even though they wanted to flee.

A hint of a smile danced across Bastion's face, there and gone in an instant. He knew full well what he was doing to me, and he was doing it on purpose. Jerk.

'I love pink.' He winked.

I felt myself flush. I'd walked right into that double entendre. I hastily changed the topic. 'Lay your hoop at the top of the pentagram then stand in the centre of the pentagram. When I tell you to – and not before – step out of it and into the protective ring. Clear?'

'Yes.' He nodded briskly, all traces of humour gone; he wanted to be rid of the curse. He laid the hoop down as I'd directed and stood in the centre of the pentagram. No emotion showed on his face, though I had no doubt he felt uneasy – most people did. When he was inside my pentagram, I could do a whole lot of malicious things to him if I wanted to. Unfortunately, my mum had raised me right. Our powers are always used to help others – the day I raise my paintbrush to kill another will be the day I give up magic and run away to join the Other Circus, forsaking the Other realm.

I placed my hoop at the base of the pentagram and stepped into it, sat down cross-legged and summoned my magic within me. Softly, I whispered, '*Isa*,' the runic word of power and touched the rune at the base of the pentagram at the same time. *Isa* can be used either to activate or to send something into stasis, depending on your potion and your intent. That is why only a few living witches attain rune mastery like I have; it is a complex, arcane art and not for the faint-hearted. It is far more common for witches to specialise in just one area of rune work, like warding or scrying or healing.

I tugged on my magic and pulled it from me, then pushed it forward so it flowed into the runes. One by one, they lit up like a string of pulsing lights.

Bastion stiffened and a low groan escaped his lips – a lesser man would have been screaming. The runes pulsed and Bastion's head was thrown back, eyes to the ceiling. Black smoke started to pour out of his eyes and the stench of rotting death filled the room. I struggled not to gag on it, but my focus had to be on him.

I watched him intently until the last tendril of foul blackness left his eyes and swirled around the room, looking for another living entity to occupy. 'Into the hoop – now!' I barked.

Bastion obeyed instantly. Copying me, he stepped into the hoop and sat down. It didn't take long for the curse to find the only other living, unprotected thing in the room. It danced towards my plant and we watched as the blackness soaked into the vibrant green shrub. In less than a minute the plant started to shrivel and die. It didn't have Bastion's magic reserves to help it survive for long.

Bastion had battled the curse for weeks – I'd never seen someone survive a black curse for so long – but now he was free of it. I had expected to feel bitter that his death was no longer a certainty but instead I felt lighter. I knew that Mum wouldn't have approved of keeping the curse on him; black magic is wrong, no matter whom it is used on.

Bastion's head slumped to his chest and he took a few deep breaths. I stood up, collected the dead plant and bagged it up to send to the cremator. The black magic was gone; it had succeeded in causing death and now it was dissipating, but I always take a belt-and-braces approach to such things.

Bastion struggled to his feet but he still looked like a faint breeze would push him over. Even so, there was something else within him now, an edge that had been missing. It was like thinking you were in a field with a castrated bull only to discover that it definitely still had its meat and two veg.

He swayed on his feet. 'Are you all right?' I asked reluctantly. He was in my room and it would be inconvenient if he KO'd here.

'Ah, Amber, I didn't know you cared.' His voice was soft, his head still lolling against his chest.

You give an inch — he takes a mile. I folded my arms. 'I don't, but I have stuff to do and playing nursemaid to you isn't on my list.'

'I'm always willing to play doctors and nurses.'

I narrowed my eyes. 'Well obviously, I'd be the doctor.'

He lifted his head and that faint smile of his appeared. 'Of course you would. I have no issue being the nurse.'

I had nothing to say to that. Nothing. I changed the subject. 'You'll need someone to take you home.'

'Arrangements have been made. Just give me a minute. All of that exhaustion has snapped into place. For the first time in weeks, I know that if I close my eyes I'll be able to sleep.'

'Not in my circle you won't!' I squawked. 'At least get onto the sofa so I can clean the pentagram.' I didn't want the bloodwork lingering any longer than necessary.

Bastion obligingly fell to his knees and crawled out of the circle. Seeing such a strong man reduced to crawling made me feel odd. He heaved himself onto the sofa, stretched out, and passed out instantly. Damn it, he hadn't even taken off his shoes; If he got mud on the sofa, he'd be paying for the upholstery to be cleaned.

I busied myself with the clean-up, washing the floor and the bloodwork bowl and getting everything back into its proper state. I put my hula hoops back in the cupboard then stared at the deadly griffin passed out on my sofa. After a moment's debate, I tugged off his shoes and set them down by the front door.

It looked like Bastion's day was over but, tired as I was, I knew that mine had barely started.

Chapter 7

I had an interview scheduled for 5pm and fifteen minutes to prepare for it. My preparation didn't include looking at the candidate's job application or his qualifications but painting truth runes on the chair on which he'd be sitting. I renew these runes monthly.

I painted and activated them carefully; I maintain the runes so that they're not strong enough to force a visitor to tell the truth but they're powerful enough to make them feel distinctly uncomfortable about lying. If my interviewee started to shift around in his seat, I'd know he was telling porkies. I had been forced to stand on truth runes myself, far stronger ones painted in blood, and I hated the overwhelming compulsion to answer any question that was asked of me. Not only was it unsubtle and rude, it was also using a sledgehammer to crack a walnut.

I waited for the runes to dry before concealing them with a seat cushion; there was no need to waste extra magic making them invisible when a cushion would do. Keep it simple, stupid.

My interviewee, Edward Tenby, was a wizard. He had already had a first interview with Jeb and Ethan and he'd passed their rigorous selection process; now the final yea or nay came down to me. The position Tenby was applying for was similar to Oscar's: driver and protector to one of our top witches – one witch in particular. I would introduce them at the end of the interview if I liked the cut of his jib.

Promptly at five, Venice Bellington escorted Edward Tenby into my room. He gave me a reserved smile and shook my hand firmly. Handsome, with a strong jaw and a cleft chin, he was at least six feet tall and his flame-red hair was the same shade as mine. It was cropped short, giving him a military appearance; that was unsurprising since he had spent four years in the Army. His handshake was firm but not crushing.

I jerked my head to the door, indicating to Venice that she should leave. She gave me a glare – I had demoted her daughter, after all – but then she tossed her blonde hair over her shoulder and sent a well-practised flirtatious pout to Tenby. I glared at her and she flounced off. I suppressed a grimace of distaste at her unprofessional behaviour in the workplace and made a mental note to have words with her later. Making kissy faces at potential new hires was *not* okay.

I smiled tightly at Tenby and apologised for Venice's behaviour but he waved it away. I gestured to the seat, and when he was safely ensconced I started the interrogation.

After an hour of probing and invasive questions, I was satisfied that he would make an excellent addition to the team. He hadn't shifted in his seat once and he came across as reliable and honest. I would give him a three-month trial before he became a permanent member of the coven's roster. I picked up the phone and dialled reception, asking them to send in Hannah Lions.

Hannah knocked on the door and entered promptly when I told her to. Not yet thirty but full of potential, she was fresh-faced and full of optimism and zeal. Like me, Hannah showed promise in using both potions *and* runes, a rare talent that must be cultivated. I noted approvingly that she'd plaited her mousy brown hair to keep it out of the way; hair in potions is an unmitigated disaster.

Her body was softly rounded giving her curves in the right places, but I was pleased to note that Tenby's eye's stayed firmly on her face.

'Edward, this is Hannah, Hannah this is Edward. We're looking at hiring Edward as your driver.' I used their first names to create a friendly connection between them; a witch and her driver need to have a strong working relationship.

She beamed at him and held out her hand. He took it with a small smile. He continued to study her but there was no spark of interest that I needed to concern myself with. Good. Relationships with your protector are never a good idea.

'Edward, the coven would like to offer you a permanent position after an initial three-month probationary period. If you would like to join us, you will need to sign a magically-enforced confidentiality contract today. Do you have an issue with that?'

'No, ma'am.'

'Excellent.' I pulled a pre-prepared contract out of my drawer, filled in his name and the date and passed it to him for signing.

He pulled out his own pen and signed with a flourish. 'Thank you for this opportunity.'

I nodded. We'd already covered that he was available to start immediately so I saw no reason to delay the start of his employment. 'Please report to the reception desk tomorrow at 9am,' I requested. 'Hannah, escort him out, then meet me in the garage,'

She nodded and stood up. One of the reasons I liked Hannah was because she didn't waste time on meaningless chatter. I had questioned her intensely on my runed chair, and I was sure that she wasn't the black witch operating out of my coven. If I'd had time, I'd have interviewed every single coven member on my chair, but it was difficult to do that with any subtlety and it wasn't a foolproof method. Truth runes can be subverted if the witch is prepared. All that aside, Hannah remained one of the few that I trusted – as much as I trusted anyone. She was eager to please and her underlying need to prove herself was something that I recognised from my own reflection in the mirror.

Her familiar, a blue corn snake, was wound around her wrist, happily snoozing. On its head was a small rune that kept it hidden from casual observers. I could only see Fifi because I already knew about her and I was looking for her. I'm not a fan of anything reptilian so I try to keep my distance from Fifi without being obvious about it; it wouldn't do for my weakness to become known. That's the sort of thing that ends with you being tortured in a pit of snakes.

I headed straight to the garage and raised an eyebrow at the griffin leaning against my car. He looked glum, like someone had stolen his favourite teddy bear. Shirdal is actually one of the few people in this realm that I truly like, despite the fact that he heads the griffin guild of assassins and *should* be persona non grata. If you thought that Shirdal was a rogue you wouldn't be wrong, but he's an affable one. We've been through many a sticky situation together and, frankly, if I had to have a griffin bodyguard he would have been my first choice all day long. He thinks that he is funnier than he is, but his heart is in the right place. And he would be a million times better than having Bastion tailing me.

As always, Shirdal was dressed like a bum: his shirt was rumpled, his trousers had mud on them and his hair was sticking up in various directions. What was unusual was his expression. He looked morose.

'Crikey,' I commented, suddenly worried. 'Who died?' My heart stopped for a moment – not Jinx or Emory surely? Jinx is one of the few people in my life that I count as a friend even though she is relatively new to the Other realm. She is a PI. With her empathy and in-built lie-detector, she'd landed on her feet and promptly met and fallen in love with Emory Elite, the king of the dragon-shifters. Jinx is pretty much my only friend these days, though I'd recently spent a good deal of time with Lucy, an alpha werewolf, and she had also grown on me. I have to admit to liking Emory too; he is a good man and he adores Jinx. For him, her happiness is paramount and that was an attitude I could get behind.

Shirdal huffed. 'Everyone's alive. Annoyingly so.'

Thank the Goddess. 'So why the long face?'

He glared. 'I'm a griffin, not a centaur!'

A horse joke. Hilarious. 'Yeah, yeah. Why are you moody?'

'An elite group of dark seraph are guarding Jinx and Emory while they are on their honeymoon.' The dark seraph is the name for the made-brethren. They had once been grotesque gargoyles, but when they were being wiped out Emory had supplanted their failing magic with his own. That had bonded them to him, and they had become his very own fanatical servants. Their bodies had morphed and changed with this new magic, and they had become human-like with huge black wings. Like I said, Emory is a good man.

'So?'

'So.' Shirdal folded his arms. 'Reynard is with them.'

'Oh.' Reynard and Shirdal had barely had a chance to connect as lovers before Jinx and Emory set off for their travels in Thailand. They'd delayed their honeymoon by a week or two while they'd put some plans in place, and then they'd jetted off without so much as a ta-ta. 'I didn't realise they were taking anyone with them.'

Shirdal smiled for the first time. 'Nor did they.'

'Uh-oh. Hidden bodyguards? Jinx is going to hit the roof when she finds out,' I warned.

'I tried to alert Reynard, but you know how the made-brethren are.'

I did. When Emory had saved them, he had not anticipated the adoration that would ensue. He now had a host of very willing, very dedicated, very zealous servants. Hence tracking the newlyweds on their honeymoon.

'That's going to blow up in Reynard's face,' I said. 'Jinx will be really mad. Her privacy is important to her.'

'I know, and so does Reynard, but their safety is paramount to him. Their happiness is secondary.'

'So you're mooning after Reynard.'

'You bet I am! No one can swear like him. He makes me look like a fucking amateur.' True: Reynard swears worse than a sailor and a soldier combined.

I rolled my eyes. 'You do *not* need to emulate him, thank you very much.'

'You don't know how to have fun.'

'I do!' I protested. I created my own potions *and* I read steamy romance novels, though I wasn't going to tell him that. 'Anyway, why are you here?'

'To protect you, of course. With Bastion out for the count, he's arranged for me to step into the breach.'

I nodded curtly, but inwardly I was pleased. If I had to have a guardian, let it be Shirdal. I hoped that Bastion would be out of commission for several weeks to come.

Hannah approached us. She had slung on a tote bag rather like my own, and she was in jeans and a jacket. She was ready to work. 'Into the car,' I said, and she slid in without comment. 'Will you be aerial or in the car?' I asked Shirdal.

'In the car.'

'Okay.' I hesitated. Our next location was one of my many secrets but Shirdal would need to know about it. 'We're visiting the Other Circus.'

I waited for questions but none came; instead, Shirdal simply nodded. There was no hint of curiosity in his face and I suddenly recalled that he had been helping out Jinx. 'You know about the Other Circus?' I asked, resignedly.

'The super-secret circus for people who want to run away from the magical realm and who then exist in the Common realm for the rest of their days? *That* super-secret circus?'

'Yes. That super-secret circus.' I sighed. 'Is it too much to ask that you make sure this doesn't become common knowledge?'

'Jinx made me swear an oath to keep it secret, so it will be.' Shirdal sounded mildly affronted. Great job, Amber: piss off the head of the assassins' guild. I should have had more faith in Jinx; of course she would keep the circus safely hidden.

'Fine. Let's go.'

Shirdal slid into the front of the car with Oscar and I got into the back with Hannah. Hannah was a very bright witch; if I became the next Symposium member, then I would need someone like her to take over running the underground movement known as the Other Circus. Succession planning is important.

I couldn't run the underground when I was officially working for the Connection. Half the reason that the Other Circus exists is to circumvent the Connection; if you need to disappear from the authorities, the circus is the place you go. Not every person becomes a part of it – some just pass through – but many find freedom and joy in travelling around with others who had similarly renounced their magic, those who understood what it was like to live forever in the Common Realm but always long for the magical one.

During the journey I asked Hannah to swear an oath of silence. 'What is forfeit?' she asked nervously.

'If you break the oath?' She nodded. 'Your life,' I said simply.

She licked her suddenly parched lips but nodded again.

'You can't tell a soul about where you're going or what you're doing. Not now, probably not ever. But you'll be doing good work.'

'Ok, Coven Mother. I'll do it.' She recited the vow of silence.

'So mote it be,' I said, witnessing her vow.

She glowed slightly as the vow took hold. I hope she didn't talk in her sleep; that would be a bitch of a way to die.

Chapter 8

Our trip to the circus was uneventful. I introduced Hannah to the circus master, Cain Stilwell. Cain's real name is Clark Farrier. In the past he was a werewolf rights activist, but he'd made too much noise and became a target for assassination. Like Jake, Clark had faked his own death but unlike Jake, rather than go into hiding in solitude with only me for company, Clark had changed his name to Cain and joined the circus.

I believe that if I'd known about the circus earlier, Jake might still be with us. It was one of the reasons I was passionate about the project that I'd inherited from Abigay. Giving people somewhere to go when they inadvertently strolled into someone's crosshairs was important.

Cain had joined the circus whilst it was under Abigay's care and he'd taken over its day-to-day running when the previous circus master retired. Hannah didn't need to know any of that; to her, he was just Cain.

I showed Hannah the runes that were crudely painted on each caravan door and taught her how they worked together to form a warding barrier at night. During the day the runes were deliberately misaligned so that anyone Other could still come to the shows and not realise that there was anything magical about them.

We'd arrived deliberately late so that I could show her all of the runes working together. Because so many people came and went, they needed to be renewed every month for maximum efficacy. It was a huge task and it normally took me a full day to complete; bringing Hannah on board would halve that time. Once I was sure she was competent, I could leave it entirely to her. Delegation doesn't come naturally to me but I was trying because the one thing I was in short supply of was time.

Cain had also asked that we help one of his trapeze artists who'd landed badly and would be out of action until he was healed magically or recovered naturally. Magic was better – and significantly faster. I was feeling tired after all I'd done and thinking longingly of my bed, so I let Hannah take point on the healing. She sorted him out quickly and efficiently, and with a far warmer bedside manner than mine. My attitude is that they don't need cuddling, they need potions and runes, but her style of healing worked just as well. Each to their own.

The drive home was silent and I struggled not to fall asleep. Luckily I held onto my dignity until I bade Hannah goodnight as the car drew in at midnight. Shirdal left too, presumably because we had already reached the safety of the coven.

Oscar escorted me to my flat. Knowing there was a black witch in our midst was making him more cautious than usual, but for once I was too weary to feel outraged that my home didn't feel safe any longer. Since we were alone, I gave him a quick kiss on the cheek before turning in. He ruffled my hair, which made me roll my eyes; he'd been doing that since I was a teen, knowing he would get a rise out of me. I'd long since given up reacting but he still did it, and secretly I liked it. He loved me. It was nice that someone did.

Oscar did a spot-check, moving room to room, making sure that the flat really was empty before he said goodnight. Bastion was no longer snoozing on my sofa but I couldn't muster the energy to wonder how he'd left. He couldn't have recovered from the curse that quickly so Shirdal must have arranged for him to be moved somewhere safe while he got better. I could only hope that it would take weeks. Maybe I could complete my potion before he came back. But then again, optimism is the master of crushing disappointment.

I woke in the morning, dead-limbed and still tired. I wanted another hour's sleep but I was itching to get started on my potion and the easiest way to do that was by creating extra time and getting up early. Again. Plus, coffee would help.

I stumbled into my lounge and stifled a scream when I saw an intruder in my kitchen. 'Fudge!' I swore.

'Fudge?' Bastion obviously found my choice of curse words amusing.

'What are you doing here?' I snarled, my heart racing.

'I'm doing my job. You hired me to protect you. I'm here to do just that.'

'Let's be clear, *I* didn't hire you. The coven council did, against my wishes. And I don't need you to protect me in my own living room. What are you going to protect me from? Bad TV choices?'

'Do you think the assassins will just pick you off at your office?' He raised one elegant eyebrow.

Damn him. He was looking well. Absurdly so. He was an attractive man, and even at his worst with huge bags beneath his eyes he'd looked better than your average Joe, but now he was almost vibrating with energy. His frame seemed bigger, broader, and he took up more space than he'd seemed to yesterday. There was a potency to him – he'd been dangerous yesterday but he was deadly today. My mouth went dry.

Forcing myself to turn my back on him, I put on the kettle. You can't show fear in this realm or they know you're weak. I concentrated on making coffee, not on the fact that his muscle mass seemed to have doubled overnight.

I pulled out one of my favourite mugs. It had a cartoon picture of a desert island on it and the words: *Sometimes you just meet someone … and you instantly realise you want to spend your whole life **without** them.* I spooned in instant coffee granules – instant coffee wasn't my favourite choice but I needed caffeine. Then I belatedly realised that I was being rude. Murderous griffin or not, my mum would kill me if I didn't offer refreshments to a guest or a contract worker.

'Coffee?' I offered weakly.

'Tea, if you're making a hot drink.'

I had very obviously just made myself a coffee, so I reluctantly prepared a mug of tea and plonked it in front of him with ill grace. The cup had a picture of a dictionary on it and the sentence: *There are 600,000 words in the English dictionary but none describe how much I wish to hit you with a chair right now.*

'Thank you.' He read the cup and his lips twitched with amusement. His eyes flicked to the nearest chair and back to me. Everything about his body language said 'go on, I dare you'. Yeah. I wasn't that stupid.

I sat opposite him and drank my coffee so fast that the hot liquid burned my throat. The urge to flee was strong now that Bastion was back in full predator mode. 'I'm going to shower,' I said casually, partly to make sure he didn't stumble into my bathroom by mistake and partly to make sure he didn't think I was leaving the room because he was making me uncomfortable. He was, but he didn't need to know that.

I showered and runed before dressing for the day. The coffee had blasted away half of the cobwebs and the shower destroyed the rest. I checked the time: 6am. I had at least three hours before people started ringing me and asking me for favours.

I looked at myself in the bathroom mirror and said my morning affirmation. 'It doesn't matter that you don't have a familiar. You are a strong, successful witch. You don't need anyone.' I spoke the words more quietly than usual – I didn't want Bastion to overhear something so intensely personal. I've been doing affirmations since I was eight; Mum had strongly believed in the power of self-belief and I was moulded in her image. She'd told me there was nothing I couldn't achieve with hard work, and even now I believed her.

I studied Bastion openly as I walked past him to get into my office. 'You recovered from the curse very quickly,' I commented.

He grinned. 'I've always been a man that recovers quickly.' He ended the comment with a wink, making me roll my eyes at his innuendo. He had clearly decided that he was going to embarrass me as retribution for me holding out on him over breaking the curse. Sucks to be him; his innuendos had no effect on me.

I hustled into my office and worked for forty minutes, poring over some old potion texts. A message arrived from Oscar: *Want to visit your mum?* I rubbed my tired eyes. I wanted to continue working on my potion but it was hard to focus with the griffin prowling next door. I'd get used to him but it would take a bit of time – and I did want to see Mum. I always do.

I responded in the affirmative and put a few sealed potion jars and some paintbrushes of various sizes into my black tote bag. Just in case. 'Let's go,' I said to Bastion.

'Where?'

'To see my mum.'

He nodded. Did he know about her circumstances, or would I have to explain about the disease that was slowly stealing her from me? I felt papery today, thin and delicate and easily ripped, so I said nothing. I didn't need to set my face to mildly bitchy because I always have a resting witch face.

I walked out of my flat without a backward glance at him. The skin between my shoulder blades itched as I went down the stairs, so even though Bastion's footfalls were silent I knew he was following me to the garage. Oscar was already there with the car engine on, warming it up for us. I slid into the back and Bastion sat next to me.

Belatedly I realised I'd better introduce them. 'Oscar, this is Bastion. Bastion, this is my wizard bodyguard, Oscar.' Bastion needed no further introduction; he is the paramount assassin of the griffins and his deadly reputation is global. As far as I knew, he only had the one name; he didn't need a second.

They exchanged brief nods and we set off in silence. I wondered if Bastion's presence was offensive to Oscar, as if it suggested that the coven thought he couldn't do his job properly. I winced; I should probably have been a bit more sensitive to Oscar's feelings when I was introducing them – but sensitivity to others' feelings isn't one of my strong points.

I missed Shirdal; if he'd been there, he would have filled the uncomfortable silence with inane chat and ill-advised jokes. 'Shirdal?' I asked Bastion laconically.

'He's on another job now that I've recovered,' he explained.

I nodded and we fell silent again. I was trying not to feel rather put out. Shirdal is a friend of mine – kind of – and he knew that I was supposedly being targeted by an assassin, but he'd left me in Bastion's tender hands. If my friend Jinx – or even Lucy – were in danger, I wouldn't leave their side until that danger was gone. But maybe friendship meant something else to me because I had so few friends. I guess if you're popular it is hard to keep all your friends safe, especially in the Other realm where danger lurks in every corner.

It was still dark and shadows clung to the car. I guess that was how the vampyr phased right in.

Chapter 9

I screamed at the sudden intrusion. Oscar spun the car around, making the vampyr stumble even as he lurched towards me. His fangs were protruding from an impossibly perfect mouth. That I could note how handsome he was as he moved to kill me showed how hard up I was. Goddess, was I so alone that his hands on me were better than nothing?

The vampyr's head jerked towards my throat but the runes there sent him reeling back, straight into Bastion's arms. Without changing expression, Bastion ripped the vampyr's head clean off of his shoulders. Black blood sprayed the inside of the car.

I stared, open-mouthed. Bastion had torn the vampyr's head from his shoulders without using a weapon, just his hands. Yikes. I hadn't doubted his reputation, but the blood that now covered me cemented it.

That was when I realised that Bastion had coolly watched as the vampyr came in for the attack. 'You're supposed to save me!' I said, a shade hysterically. 'You waited until he attacked me!'

Bastion waved away my objection. 'You weren't in any real danger. I wanted to see what protective runes you had on you.'

'You could have just *asked!*'

'And would you have been honest?'

About the protections I runed on every day? No, of course not – I wasn't going to tell the griffin something that he might use later to attack me. My silence was answer enough.

'Exactly,' he said, looking at me grimly.

The vampyr's body disintegrated into a cloud of ash and Oscar discreetly opened all the windows. When he had spun the car around, he'd slammed on the brakes ready to swivel in his seat and use the IR to come to my aid. He hadn't needed to because Bastion got there first.

Bastion looked comfortable. A small intimate smile was playing at the corner of his mouth and he looked as relaxed as a man who had just copulated. I had a sudden image of him lying in bed smoking a cigarette with that same half-smile. Death was its own release to him, and I wondered if griffins even cared about sex if that was how killing someone made them feel. It was not a question I would ever ask in this lifetime.

Oscar started the car again, which broke the staring competition that had developed between Bastion and me.

The dust was swirling in the air. I covered my nose and mouth with a handful of my heavy black skirt so that I didn't accidentally inhale any of the asshole who'd tried to kill me. Unfortunately his blood splatter hadn't disintegrated like the rest of him and I was covered in his gunk. I tried hard not to think about it; anyway, I had spare clothes in the boot of Oscar's car for just such occasions.

Suddenly my brain clicked into gear and started racing at a million miles a minute. I was a known – and welcome – associate of a number of the vampyr clans, so only a fool would try to attack me. A dead fool, as it happened. I was on my way to see Mum and someone had attacked me en route... 'Mum!' I barked urgently to Oscar. 'Step on it!'

His jaw tightened and the car leapt forward. Luckily we weren't far from the care home, and all seemed quiet when we finally screeched to a stop and ran inside.

'You cannot go in to see your mother like that!' the matron on the ward squawked at me.

I opened my mouth to argue but closed it again. She was right, I couldn't. Mum was fragile now and I couldn't possibly let her see me covered in vampyr blood. It would upset her, whether she remembered me today or not. 'You go ahead,' I ordered Oscar. 'I'll clean up.' He nodded and strode towards Mum's room.

'And that's why you need me,' Bastion murmured softly. 'He's your bodyguard but he just left you after an attack to protect your mum.'

I glared. 'I ordered him to.'

'You did – but his sole focus should be you, and it's not.'

I hated that he was criticising Oscar. Oscar was doing exactly as he should. If something happened to Mum because of me, I'd never forgive myself.

I ignored Bastion, grabbed my go-bag from the car and returned to the care home for my second shower of the day. Once I was clean, I dressed in a pale-blue peasant blouse and a black skirt that flowed around my ankles. Underneath my skirt were leggings so I could whip off the skirt and run like hell if I needed to. I was lucky I lived in a mediocre climate where I could get away with layering my clothes.

I transferred my potion bomb to my skirt pocket and fingered the vial nervously. It suddenly felt more necessary than ever; crazy as it seemed, someone really *was* trying to kill me.

I used the privacy of the shower to call Lord Volderiss, the head of all of the vampyr clans and currently the

Symposium member representing them. I had his personal number and, not caring about the early hour, I dialled it.

'Miss DeLea,' he answered smoothly. 'To what do I owe the pleasure?'

I pictured him in my mind, pale-skinned with salt-and-pepper hair – an affectation, of course, because a vampyr could appear whatever age they wished, from child to crone. Lord Volderiss had picked somewhere in between, older but not old, nor young enough to look unwise.

'I've just been attacked by a vampyr.' Despite my outrage, I tried to keep my tone even. I didn't want him to think I was accusing him of being involved or being incompetent because I didn't believe he was either.

'How unfortunate,' he murmured sympathetically, giving away nothing.

'Indeed,' I responded drily. 'Very unfortunate.' It sounded like we were talking about bad weather, not someone trying to kill me.

'Did you recognise the attacker? I assume they've been dispatched by now?' What a cold term 'dispatched' was.

'Yes, he's permanently dead,' I confirmed grimly. 'I didn't recognise him.'

'Was he wearing a clan shield?' Volderiss probed.

'No. He was dressed all in black. He was brunette and pale skinned, with no distinguishing features.' That was all I had. My attacker's age didn't matter, and *all* vampyrs are insanely good looking because something in the change burns out their imperfections. The clans are filled with examples of model-like beauty, so there was no over-large nose or overbite teeth to remember him by.

'Hmm,' Lord Volderiss murmured. 'I will make enquires, Miss DeLea, but that's not much to go on.'

It wasn't. 'If you can't find out who he is, you can send one of your vampyrs to my coven. I'll scry him from my head and your vampyr can identify him.'

Lord Volderiss laughed. 'You're not going to invite a vampyr into your coven.'

What was I thinking? Of course I couldn't. The trauma of the attack had clearly addled my thinking and that pissed me off more.

'Go to Wokeshire's while it's still fresh in your mind,' Volderiss suggested. 'He'll be able to identify him or pass the image to me for me to do so.'

'Fine. Tell him to expect me.'

'When?'

'Imminently.'

I hung up impatiently. I had to visit Mum first, but I wanted to know who was trying to kill me and to put a stop to them. I didn't want Mum to have a target on her head because of me. I'd do anything to keep her safe, even if it meant working with vampyrs – or worse, Bastion.

Chapter 10

Bastion was leaning against the wall waiting for me. He said nothing when I left the bathroom. My turn, then. 'I want a griffin to protect my mum round the clock, like you've got me.'

He raised an eyebrow. 'I've got you, have I? Lucky me.'

I glared and he held his hands up in surrender. 'We're assassins, not bodyguards,' he explained.

'If you can assassinate, you can protect. Same skillset,' I argued.

'Very much opposing skillsets.' He sent me an amused look that lit fury in my veins.

'If this is a joke to you, then you can go—'

The amusement leached out of his eyes. 'I'm sorry, witch. I am taking this seriously but I can't resist riling you. You get like a cat, hissing at me with all your fur standing on end. It's cute.'

Cute? *Cute?* I'd give him cute!

He held a hand up before I could blister him with my righteous rage. 'I'm good at keeping people safe. I kept Jessica Sharp safe for years without her knowledge. But I'm rare. Most griffins go in, slice a throat and leave and that's not what you need right now.'

'I need someone to guard my mother.'

'You need someone unobtrusive,' he clarified. 'Leave it with me. Go see your mum while I make some calls.'

After all his negative comments about Oscar, I was surprised he was letting me out of his sight. 'Don't you think you should be in the same room as me?' I snarked.

'You'll have Oscar in the room and I'll be just outside of the door if you need me.'

'I'll never need you.' I marched in without looking back.

Because I was in a snit, my brain wasn't quite engaged. When I saw my mother smiling at Oscar with love in her eyes, I automatically greeted her without thinking. 'Hi, Mum.'

She turned to me and frowned in confusion. 'You're not my daughter. My daughter is ten.' She turned to Oscar. 'Who is this?'

My heart froze and my stomach lurched. So it was my turn, then: my turn to be forgotten.

Oscar turned sympathetic eyes on me. 'Someone I work with,' he said simply. He took her hand and re-directed her attention back to him.

I sat in the chair by the window, giving them a little space. I couldn't bring myself to leave just yet. After the scare in the car, I needed to see her even if she didn't really see me.

I listened as Oscar told Mum a little about the previous day; he edited his account but he still wanted to share his life with her as much as he could. They only spoke for half an hour but by the end Mum was looking pale and lost.

'Lucille,' I called to her familiar. 'Can you help her?'

The black-and-white ferret had been snoozing by Mum's feet, but she stirred and stretched as I called her name. Whether Mum knew me or not, Lucille always did and she came to me for a stroke.

'How peculiar,' Mum murmured, looking at her familiar in surprise.

'Animals like me,' I said hastily. 'It must be a pheromone thing.'

Lucille chittered at me. After I stroked her head she happily bounced her way over to Mum. She leapt up onto her lap before making the last climb onto her shoulders and settling in by her neck.

Lucille glowed slightly as she touched her little pink nose to Mum's skin and my mother visibly relaxed. Her skin took on a healthy rosy hue as Lucille sent her extra strength and energy. Finally the ferret familiar removed her nose, yawned showing short spikey teeth, snuggled down and promptly went back to sleep.

Most familiars don't need touch to help their witch but as Mum got ill, the bond between her and Lucille was the first thing to be strained. Lucille could still help, but it took a bigger toll on her too and I felt bad for asking. Still, it was a relief to see Mum looking a little more vibrant because I hated seeing her vulnerable and lost. It is the natural way of things for a child to look after their parent, I told myself firmly. But natural as it might be, I had no siblings to ease the burden. I was grateful for Oscar.

I let them speak for a few minutes more before I cleared my throat. I had Wokeshire waiting for me and a killer vampyr to identify. Oscar met my eyes and nodded. He never once gave the impression that he minded being at my beck and call, but I instantly regretted pulling him away from Mum. 'Bastion could take me?' I offered quietly.

'No.' He forced a smile. 'It's okay.' He leaned forward and kissed Mum on the forehead. 'I'll see you again soon, Luna,' he promised warmly.

I felt a pang. Who knew if she would remember either of us tomorrow? Oscar should be making the most of the today's lucidity. 'Stay,' I entreated.

He shook his head. 'We have things to do.'

Luna smiled. 'Of course you do. You're a sexy wizard with important duties. Come here, stud muffin. Give me a proper farewell kiss.' She reached behind his neck and pulled him down. I resisted the urge to moan 'ewwwww' as I had done as a teenager.

When she pulled away, she was smiling and my heart warmed. She fixed me with sharp eyes. 'Has the Prophecy come to pass yet, Am?'

The smile dropped from my face. This wasn't the first time she'd mentioned a prophecy to me.

'What prophecy?' I asked urgently.

She blinked and the moment was gone. So was she. 'I have no idea what you're talking about.' She frowned. 'You'll keep my Oscar safe, won't you?'

I nodded, my heart still racing. I swallowed hard. 'I will,' I promised, and I meant it with all my heart.

Chapter 11

Lord Wokeshire frowned at the image that was floating in the scrying bowl. 'I don't know him.'

'Now you never will,' I said drily. I focused on holding the vampyr's image in my mind. It is all but impossible to self-scry, so I'd summoned Hannah and Tenby to meet us at Wokeshire's residence. Hannah had carried out the rune work without the slightest hint of trepidation at being within the vampyrs' nest. Tenby was visibly on guard but not offensively so.

'Get a photo of this image,' Wokeshire barked at a lackey.

Someone stepped forward and I concentrated on holding the image nice and clear until the pictures were taken. 'Send the photo to Volderiss,' Wokeshire ordered. 'I will make my own enquiries, Miss DeLea.'

I gestured for Hannah to break the scry. As she painted *ezro*, a headache slammed into me. A scry headache is almost migraine territory and I worked to keep the sudden pain off my face. Hannah started clearing up and passed me some paracetamol and ibuprofen, which I swallowed gratefully. Healing potions have no effect on a scry headache but good old Common-realm medicine would soon have me feeling better.

Wokeshire cleared his throat. 'Whilst I have you here, I wonder if *you* could assist with a little matter?' Although he was calling it a little matter, his body language said otherwise; he was tense and struggling to hide it. The emphasis on *you* told me that it was something for me to handle rather than Hannah.

I nodded and turned to Hannah and Tenby. 'Good work. Return to the tower.'

'Thank you, Coven Mother.' Hannah gave me a respectful bow before she turned away with Tenby at her heels.

I turned back to Wokeshire. 'I will assist you if I can. Tell me about the problem.'

'One of my vampyrs has been injured – a cut that seems to have become infected.'

I frowned. 'And your spit hasn't resolved it?'

Wokeshire grimaced. The fact that vampyr spit can heal cuts is supposed to be a secret, but like most of the secrets in the Other realm it is pretty much common knowledge, especially to witches and healing wizards.

'No. The wound tastes foul and the one that licked it has also fallen ill.'

Spitting directly in a wound, as opposed to licking it, is considered a grave insult. The only exception is when healing a wizard and that is only because consuming witches' blood sends vampyrs loopy. A vampyr high on wizard's blood has to be put down or stopped before they tear through the human population. That's why I had alerted the proper authorities after the vampyr attack the other night. Wizard blood is bad news for them – and the withdrawal from it is even worse. Force-feeding a misbehaving vampyr wizard blood and then watching them jones for more is a rather brutal method of torture that the older vampyrs still employ occasionally – despite the fact that it is completely forbidden.

I shouldered my tote bag. 'Show me.'

Keeping half an eye on Bastion, Wokeshire escorted me down to the dungeons. His lackeys blustered around him, keeping their fangs out in clear threat. Bastion looked amused; they weren't a threat to him.

Bastion has a rare magical gift: he can *coax*. He can force someone into a course of action; as long as they have the slightest inclination to do something, he can amplify that urge and make them do it – like making all the little vampyrs flee. I had no doubt that the urge to run was present in each of them and they looked petrified. Bastion has a towering reputation. They say he's the deadliest assassin to have ever walked the Earth. I sniffed. He is a knob.

Two cells were occupied by vampyrs lying prone on uncomfortable looking beds. As I stepped forward, one of them sat up and hissed at me like a cat. His eyes were black. Uh-oh.

As I moved closer, they both ran forward to cling to the metal bars. I surreptitiously checked the runes I'd painted on the dungeon walls during another visit but thankfully they were all in good condition. I relaxed. The containment runes were still holding strong so, much as these two vampyrs clearly wanted to attack me, they couldn't phase into the shadows and out at me. It had been more than a month since I'd last runed it, which showed that Lord Wokeshire wasn't one of the vampyr lords who regularly chucked his vampyrs into the dungeons. Good for him; you always get better results with a carrot rather than a stick.

When I glanced at Wokeshire, I was surprised by the sorrow on his face. He obviously thought the two vampyrs were a lost cause and I wasn't sure he was wrong. I'd only seen vampyrs act like this once before, and that was when they were being controlled by a witch so black that she'd tipped into necromancer territory.

Whoever had done this had nowhere near her expertise; this was someone dabbling – and doing it badly. They'd tried to take over one of the vampyrs, probably with a potion on a blade, which would have been easier than getting the vampyr to willingly imbibe it. They'd got a two-for-one special because the other one was infected from licking the wound.

'When did their eyes change?' I asked.

'They were normal when I came down this morning,' Wokeshire replied grimly. 'Necromancy,' he spat. All vampyrs hate necromancers. Necromancers specialise in animating the dead and, since vampyrs are dead men walking, they take that kind of thing personally.

'Incompetent necromancy,' I corrected. 'Normally when a necromancer seizes control of a vampyr it's an instant hold. This is a slow leech.'

'What does that mean?'

'It means we might be able to stop it,' I said with more confidence than I felt.

Wokeshire's shoulders dropped in relief. 'Whatever you need, I'll make sure you get it. Please, Miss DeLea. This is my daughter's husband.' He gestured to the man in front of me, though I noted that he barely glanced at the second guy who was obviously dispensable.

'We've got time on our side. I'll go home and see if I can brew a counter potion. It's a good thing they didn't imbibe the black witch's potion. This way we have a fighting chance. I'll need a sample of each of their blood.' A thought suddenly occurred to me. 'The vampyr that attacked me this morning, were his eyes black? I didn't notice.'

'He definitely had dark eyes.' Wokeshire frowned and clicked his fingers at one of his lackeys. 'Show me the image.'

The minion leapt forward eagerly, pulled his phone from his pocket and retrieved the image of the vampyr. Bastion, Lord Wokeshire and I stared at it.

'Maybe,' Wokeshire said finally. 'The shadows in the car make it difficult to tell for sure.' That, and the fact that scrying an image could only show what I could recall. It didn't mean it was completely accurate. I have a good memory but not an eidetic one.

'I'll go and start the potion. I'll need that blood now,' I instructed.

'I'll harvest it myself.'

'Don't. These two are clearly contagious, though hopefully only if you imbibe their blood, but it's best not to take chances.'

He nodded reluctantly. 'Fine. One of my men will get the blood for you. Will you wait upstairs?'

'We'll wait in our car,' I said firmly. Although I had plenty of vampyr allies, the attack was still fresh in my mind so I wasn't keen on lounging around surrounded by a whole clan of them.

'How long will it take? The potion?' Wokeshire asked.

'I already have one brewing with a solid base that I should be able to amend. A few hours, if I can get it right. A day, if I have to start over.' I pointed to the two black-eyed vampyrs. 'Keep them contained and isolated in the meantime.'

Wokeshire turned to the vampyrs milling around him. 'Volunteers?' Four of the five stepped back, leaving the fifth man to inadvertently volunteer. 'Good man, Kelsey.' As Wokeshire clapped him on the shoulder, panic flared in the poor guy's eyes.

'Get some blood from Kelsey, too, in case he gets infected. Then I can cure him at the same time,' I suggested.

The 'volunteer' sent me a grateful look though I didn't acknowledge his gratitude. I was just doing my job. Thinking of these things is why I earn the big bucks.

Wokeshire didn't leave us sitting in our car for long. His daughter, Mererid, came out carrying a cooler box presumably containing three vials of blood. Her hair is blonde in contrast to her father's black, and her skin is incredibly pale. No way are they biologically related, but I know better than most that it takes more than blood to make a family.

She opened the back door of the car and passed the cooler to me. 'Don't fuck this up,' she snarled.

I forgave her rudeness – she was worried about her husband – but nevertheless I gave her a hard look.

'Or you'll do what, vampyr?' Bastion's voice was low and slow. The threat was clear.

Mererid swallowed hard and suddenly looked less sure of herself. 'What's it to you?' she managed.

'She's *my* witch under *my* protection,' Bastion growled. 'Let it be known.'

Mererid ducked her head as she shut the car door. She disappeared in a moment. Vampyric speed is no joke; they make Usain Bolt look slow.

I folded my arms. 'I'm not *your* witch. I'm *a* witch.'

'You're under my protection, are you not?'

'Yes,' I agreed reluctantly.

'Then you're my responsibility until I'm ordered otherwise.'

Such a time couldn't come soon enough.

Chapter 12

I tried to leave Bastion at the coven tower's reception but he insisted on accompanying me up to my flat. It was difficult to disagree with his reasoning given that I'd been attacked in the car, but at least Oscar listened to my objections and went off to have some down time. Bastion stuck to me like stickweed, and he was just as welcome.

As we approached my front door, he gestured for me to get behind him whilst he went first. 'It's fine.' I rolled my eyes. 'No one has been in.' I nodded at the door. I live on the sixth floor and on my door is a number six. Before I left every day, I hung it upside down so it read as a nine. If no one came into my room it stayed as a nine, but if anyone touched the door the slightest movement would swing it down to a six instead. I demonstrated quickly, moving the nine back to the six position.

He stared at me. '*That's* your security?'

I huffed. 'Well, that and all the warding runes.' There were a *lot* of warding runes.

'The runes can be gotten around.' He touched the back of his left hand and the bare skin of his arm lit up with runes.

I rolled my eyes. 'These were painted by *my* staff. That's different.'

'Not if someone is betraying you, it isn't.' What an upbeat attitude. 'I'm ordering a proper security system for you.'

I opened my mouth to argue then closed it with a clack as I remembered the fear that had rushed through me as the vampyr had attacked. 'Fine. Whatever. Fill your boots. That can keep you busy while I work,' I said firmly.

Bastion went through my flat room by room, whilst I waited impatiently, tapping my toe. When he gave me the all clear, I took off my tote bag and put the potions back into the fridge to increase their longevity. Bastion watched me.

'Do your thing,' I instructed. 'Just leave me to do mine.'
'No.'
'No?'
'I'm not taking my eyes off of you.'
My mouth dropped open. 'This is ridiculous.'

'Someone just tried to kill you. You have a black witch and/or a necromancer on the loose. Do you really think betrayal is so far out of the realms of possibility?'

Damn it. When he put it that way... 'Just don't get in my way,' I snarled.

We'd been up and out before the crack of dawn and it was still only just midday. I was hungry but I didn't want to delay brewing the potion in case it went wrong and I had to start from scratch again. Despite the Common-realm medicine my head was still pounding, though it was down to a dull ache rather than a roar.

I eyed Bastion reluctantly and sighed. Whatever I thought of him, it was clear that he was smart. He'd figure out sooner rather than later that my flat didn't take up the square footage of the whole floor – it is spacious, but not *that* spacious. It was only a matter of time before he worked out there was a hidden room. I hated that he was learning all of my secrets. I'd always kept Mum's condition quiet and her location a secret but now he knew about both, and he would learn about my lab, too. I didn't like it one bit.

Ignoring him, I strode into my office though I didn't bother shutting the door behind me. What was the point? Instead I went to the bookshelf and pulled on a copy of *A Midsummer's Night Dream*. That poor man Shakespeare had accidentally discovered the Other realm, but the wizards hadn't been so efficient at wiping memories in those days and they'd left a fair bit of magic rattling around in his brain.

When I pulled on the book's spine, a door clicked open revealing my private laboratory. The potion base for my Other Realm Additional Length potion – or my ORAL potion, as I was calling it – had cooled and was in stasis. I moved a second cauldron closer and decanted half the base into it. The new potion was a healing one, so I used a pewter cauldron rather than a bronze one.

I lit the flames under the tripod and moved the half-full pewter cauldron onto it. My hidden laboratory has no windows so I slid the air vents to open.

While the potion started to warm through, I turned to the DeLea potion bible. It isn't sentient like Grimmy, but it is still incredibly useful. I paged through the worn tome until I came to the page I was looking for: a recipe for a purifying potion for expunging evil. It is usually used in daemon possessions, but I saw no reason why it couldn't be modified for the necromancer's potion. It would need more motherwort, sage and blue vervain, but I was hopeful it would work.

I stepped out of my heavy black skirt; my leggings are far more practical for potion working. The heavy skirts look the part, but it wouldn't do to trip up in the middle of a brewing session.

I tried to ignore the fact that Bastion had slipped into the room when I was stripping off my skirt. It didn't matter – I was still completely decent. It was fine.

I studiously ignored him and started brewing.

It took another four hours to get the new potion just right. I poured it into three smaller cauldrons before adding the last ingredient, the vampyr blood, to each one. When the blood hit the potion, it frothed and bubbled and black smoke billowed off it. Now each potion was keyed specifically to each vampyr. I let out a sigh of relief. It was going to work.

I made sure I had noted which blood had been added to which cauldron, then decanted the potions into glass vials and marked them accordingly. Each vial was one measure of medicine. It would take days to gradually force the necromancer's hold from the vampyrs' souls, but slow and steady was the name of the game. If I did it too quickly, the necromancer might hold shards of their soul ready to be twisted and used again.

After I'd decanted each potion into a vial, I stoppered them; that is really an acolyte's job but I'm too much of a control freak to let anyone into my laboratory. Except a certain assassin who was hard to say no to. I grimaced.

I wiped sweat from my brow; vents or not, the room was hot. The slightly foul metallic tang of the vampyrs' blood hung in the air, mixed with the herbal earthy smell of the potion. I was relieved that it was going to work, but a tad dismayed at the thought of all the work I'd have to do to create more base for my ORAL potion. Never mind: that was tomorrow-Amber's problem.

I started to walk out of the room and gasped as I saw Bastion. He'd been so silent, I'd almost forgotten he was there.

'You're good at that,' he noted.

'At what?' Being surprised?

'At making potions. You do it instinctively as well as consciously. You stop and calculate, pulling off another leaf of this, another eye of that.'

I put my hands on my hips. 'There were no eyes used in this potion.'

'I'm trying to give you a compliment.'

'I noticed and it makes me uncomfortable, so I was ignoring it. Thanks for co-operating with that,' I said drily.

He looked amused. 'Why do compliments make you uncomfortable?'

'I'm just doing my job.'

'You're saving their lives. Three of them. That's not nothing.'

'I didn't say it was *nothing*, I said it was my job.' I shrugged. 'I'm going to shower.'

I'd barely stepped under the spray when my phone rang. Muttering to myself, I turned off the water, dried my hands and answered it.

It was an air elemental, Ada Marlow, for whom I'd worked for years. She didn't wait for me to greet her before she started to wail. 'Please, Miss DeLea, Frankie is missing! Please, can you scry him?'

I knew her son well; I'd been present at his birth and I'd been Ada's healer of choice ever since. I'd been there for every scraped knee and every bump and bruise, even the ones that certainly didn't require a healer. Fortunately Ada runs her own windfarm company and she isn't strapped for cash; energy is big business, but at least hers is green. I bill her exorbitantly in the hope that she'll stop calling me for Frankie's every bump and boo-boo, but if anything it seems to have encouraged her to call me even more. I was expensive, and therefore elite.

Little Frankie Marlow was missing. My stomach lurched as I pictured the child. Dammit. Poor kid and poor Ada, but just once I wanted *someone* to ring just to say 'hi'.

'Text me the address and get an object that's dear to Frankie. I'll come myself or send someone if I can't make it,' I confirmed brusquely and disconnected the call. I knew Ada's home address but that might not be from where Frankie had gone missing.

Needing to find some fresh clothes, I left the bathroom with a towel wrapped around me. I was halfway into my bedroom when I felt Bastion's eyes on me and froze, like a mouse caught in an eagle's gaze. His eyes were brown now. I forced myself to keep walking. He'd have noticed the pause – he noticed everything – but it couldn't be helped. How could I have forgotten that Bastion was in my lounge? I would have pulled my sweaty blouse back on if I'd remembered that he was lurking there.

I dressed hastily before going into my office. I checked the coven roster on my computer and grimaced when I saw that everyone was either off duty or on a job. I rested my head on my desk and counted to five then sat up and scrubbed my eyes. Tiredness was tugging at my limbs but I couldn't leave Frankie alone and scared somewhere. And there was a tendril of fear that maybe the black witch had graduated from ravens to kids...

Chapter 13

I'd taken more paracetamol but the pounding in my head still hadn't subsided. Oscar looked as fresh as a daisy. Lucky him; he'd had some downtime while I'd been brewing like a witch possessed but I didn't begrudge him his rest.

Ada had texted me her usual home address, so I told Oscar to drive us there. I had the vampyrs' potions packed in a cooler; we'd swing by Wokeshire after we'd found little Frankie.

In my office, I'd done a quick rune toss with my private rune stones. I'd packed the potions for the scry in my trusty tote together with some healing potions in case Frankie was hurt. Bastion had followed me around like a sad puppy, silence cloaking him like a death shroud. It felt entirely too appropriate. Now he was sitting next to me in the car. I tried not to feel too jittery that another vampyr might slide into the shadows and try to bite me.

Oscar spoke into the silence. 'I had the car runed against vampyrs. Meredith did it.'

Metal doesn't hold runes well; that's why we don't routinely rune cars. The protection would fade within a day or two and have to be reapplied, and it was an unnecessary expense. However, I couldn't bring myself to admonish Oscar; he was keeping me safe. Tension left my body and I nodded my thanks.

Silence fell again. I looked out of the window and let the world go by, struggling not to be lulled to sleep by the motion of the car. Now wasn't the time for a snooze, though my body heartily disagreed. My eyelids felt heavy and I surreptitiously pinched my thigh under my voluminous skirt. The little spark of pain was enough to keep my eyes open, but only just.

The air elemental's house was a hive of activity; Ada is the queen bee in these parts and everyone was buzzing about her. Adrenaline sparked and tiredness left me. It was go-time and Frankie needed me alert and able.

We were shown into the house. If anyone found it odd that I was accompanied by an assassin, they didn't show it. In the Other realm, curiosity kills the cat and then eats it for breakfast.

Ada is no fool. A porcelain bowl and a water filter brimming with distilled water were waiting for me. She stood as I walked in, presenting me with a tear-streaked face. 'Find him, Amber,' she demanded.

Gone was the respectful 'Miss DeLea' of the phone call; she had me here now and there was no need to be polite. There was no pleading in her tone; it was an order ... and a threat. Her elemental powers were wild: her translucent hair was flying back from her face as if she were standing in front of a fan, and an icy wind was whipping around the room. I started to shiver.

'Get a hold of yourself,' I barked firmly. 'I won't have you ruin the scrying by spilling the water or knocking the bowl.' Or have me paint a rune wrongly because I was shaking so badly from the cold.

Ada took a deep breath and blew it out several times until her transparent hair settled against her shoulders and the sharp breeze stopped.

I picked up the porcelain bowl and inspected it for impurities. There appeared to be none but I cleaned it again just to be sure. I poured the pure water into the bowl and readied my potions and my brushes. 'Object,' I demanded, holding out my hand.

Ada passed a small teddy to me. I painted on *othala* for separation and *ehwaz* for progression. Next I painted on *kenaz* for guidance. Only three rune stones had fallen on the rune cloth; it was a small spread but perhaps that was more efficient for finding the child. The Goddess guides the runes and I listen; only a fool ignores the stones.

I laid the teddy into the water and guided my magic into the runes. They lit up and dropped into the water, sliding off the teddy like a temporary tattoo. I removed the teddy from the water and the runes coalesced into the centre of the bowl before showing me an image of a child. He was curled up, happily dozing, and I could see his chest rising and falling. My shoulders slumped in relief.

I pulled the vision back a little so I could see more of his location. He was beneath an outbuilding. I tried to pull back further but the vision wasn't letting me see any more. This required a more hands-on approach.

'He's fine. He's sleeping under an outbuilding. I couldn't see exactly where so I suspect he's on the property,' I stated. 'It won't take us long to find him – I still have the connection open.'

Ada collapsed in relief. 'Thank God,' she murmured and crossed herself.

One of Ada's lieutenants was handing out torches and I took one as we all left the warm house to find Frankie.

Ada's business was doing well – no surprise for an air elemental owning a wind farm – so there were six outbuildings on the gargantuan property. I strode towards the first one but it didn't have the wrap-around deck that

I'd seen in the vision so I moved on to the next. I let my gut guide me; the connection was still there between the vision and me.

I moved past the next outbuilding until I came to a larger one. It housed a swimming pool and had a large wrap-around deck full of sun-loungers and neat table and chair sets. I skirted around the back of the building with Bastion on my heels. His eyes were glowing golden and he was scanning the area around us with sharp, bird-like movements.

I found the small hole in the deck. 'Here!' I called loudly. It was incredibly small, and it was difficult to imagine even a toddler climbing down there. We wouldn't be able to crawl in after him. Bastion knelt down and grasped the surrounding boards. His arms rippled and bulged and then he tore them away effortlessly.

I shone the torch into the hole and the light hit Frankie's sandy locks. I gave a sigh of relief. He was fine; he hadn't been kidnapped by a black witch, he'd being playing hide and seek with a little too much enthusiasm.

Bastion carefully reached into the space, gently lifted out the sleeping boy and cradled him gently, careful not to wake him. Ada was running towards us and she let out a sob as she saw her son safe and sound. When she reached us, panting, Bastion gently transferred Frankie to her waiting arms. I tried not to look askance at the assassin. He had a daughter so clearly he must be capable of some sort of familial relationship, but it was jarring to see him being so gentle.

Ada kissed her son's tousled hair over and over again as we quietly made our way back into the main house. I was glad for the warmth. I hadn't dressed for an outside excursion and my skin was prickling with cold – I always feel the cold more when I'm tired. I went into the main room and carefully packed my bag and cleared up after myself. Potions could be misused in the wrong hands.

I'd had too little sleep and too much excitement. My skin was itchy, and itchy skin is the tell-tale sign that I need to go to the Common realm to re-charge my magical batteries. I hate stepping through the portal and only having the barest whisper of magic around me. In the Common, I would be unable to see enemies around me. An ogre or a griffin could be right next to me and I wouldn't know because they'd look like ordinary humans. But whether I hated it or not, today a visit was necessary. That last bit of magic had been enough to make me feel like I'd been liberally dusted with itching powder. It was only sheer strength of will that was stopping me from clawing at my skin.

I texted Maxwell, the fire elemental who runs Rosie's café, the local portal. *I need a re-charge. Do you have capacity for an overnight stay? ADL.* Then I continued to pack my potions and paintbrushes, letting the routine soothe me. I felt on edge, no doubt because my day had started so badly. Getting attacked by a vampyr had put me in a bad mood. Go figure.

I'd finished packing up and was heading into the hallway when Ada came in still carrying Frankie, though now he was awake. She was holding him tightly and scolding him loudly for scaring her. She didn't acknowledge me as she carried him up the stairs towards his bedroom. I glanced back as they went up the staircase; Frankie's T-shirt was riding up and it was by sheer luck that I saw a flash of a rune.

'Ada! Stop!' I closed the distance between us and ran up the stairs with Bastion only a step behind me. I tried to ignore him, as if he were merely a shadow. My annoying ever-present shadow.

'Hi, Ambie,' Frankie gave me a wave and affection warmed my heart.

'Hi, Frankie.' I chucked him under his chin.

'Frankie-Wankie,' he chirped back.

'We don't really say that,' I murmured as I lifted his T-shirt. One small innocuous-looking rune. Another twenty-four hours and it would have faded from sight.

'To the bathroom,' I instructed Ada sharply. We stripped Frankie and I checked him over for stray runes. There were none bar the one I'd already spotted: *isa* for stasis. I'd bet my bottom dollar that it had been painted on with an anaesthetic potion. Someone had wanted Frankie to fall asleep, though why was anyone's guess. The whole thing was utterly weird.

I wet a flannel and wiped the rune; it came off easily without the need for a cancelling rune. Whoever had painted it had relied on the potion and not used much magic to activate it. It was sloppy and lazy.

'Someone painted a little thing on your back,' I said lightly to Frankie. 'Who was it?'

'Yeah, a sparkly tattoo.' Frankie yawned.

'Who gave you the tattoo?' I pressed.

'A girl.'

At least we knew we were looking for a female. 'What did she look like?' I pressed.

'She had a hood on. I couldn't see too well.'

Ada's face darkened.

'How do you know it was a girl?' I asked.

'She sounded like one.' Frankie snuggled sleepily into his mum's arms. 'She sang me "Baby Shark". She knew all the moves.'

'He's all clear,' I murmured to Ada. 'Put him to bed, and in the morning remind him about stranger danger.'

'I'm going to find this bitch of a witch and destroy her,' she snarled. 'Don't get in my way, Amber.'

I said nothing. I didn't want to tell her that our goals were aligned.

'Let's go,' Bastion said brusquely. I deliberately moved more slowly now that he was in a hurry. Who did he think he was to order me around? He caught the obstinate look on my face. 'This may be a trap,' he murmured for my ears alone. 'For you.'

I frowned. 'What makes you say that?'

'Someone runed the kid and made him have a nap. He wasn't harmed.'

'Yeah. So?'

'So if it was really an attack on Marlow, then why wasn't the kid taken or harmed? Instead he was hidden so you'd be hired to come here and scry him. It's well known that you're Ada's witch of choice.'

'It's a bit of a stretch,' I said dubiously.

'I said it *may* be a trap – it might not be. But either way, we need to make tracks.'

I let him usher me away. It was time to get the heck out of Dodge in case he was right. And, much as I hated to admit it, it didn't feel like he was wrong.

Chapter 14

I insisted that we went to Wokeshire's as we'd planned, though Bastion was on edge the whole time. I handed the vials over to the vampyr lord personally. It transpired that Kelsey, the volunteer, had indeed been infected while retrieving the blood, though he still had his wits about him and his eyes had yet to turn black.

Luckily, we were prepared. I explained the strict potion regime they needed to use: three vials a day, exactly eight hours apart. With the volunteer still compos mentis, he could administer the potion to all three of them so no one else risked being infected.

As we were leaving, Maxwell responded that he had a space for me. It was a small flat, not the penthouse, but I could take it or leave it. I grimaced. My skin was crawling and I was exhausted; I didn't want to face the drive back, I wanted to walk through the portal and pass out.

I'll take it. See you in 10. ADL, I replied. Aloud I said to Oscar, 'Take us to Rosie's. I need a re-charge.'

Oscar grimaced and scratched his arm. 'So do I,' he admitted as he turned the car towards Rosie's.

Dammit, that was poorly timed but it couldn't be helped. At least we had Bastion to watch our backs while we were both in the Common realm. Luckily, we weren't far from the coffee-house-cum-portal-hall. I was dying to get rid of this itch, literally sitting on my hands to prevent myself from scratching because, if I started, I'd end up bleeding.

No amount of scratching alleviates the itchy feeling; it is torture. If you leave it long enough, you'll be drop-kicked out of the Other realm – portal or no – but that always comes with unconsciousness. The last thing you want is to be passed out in the Common realm in the middle of who knows where. The vulnerability of being there at all made me shudder.

Oscar parked the car outside Rosie's and I hopped out. I always have a go-bag in the boot, as does Oscar. What Bastion did was no concern of mine. I popped the boot. Huh. There was another holdall in there that I didn't recognise – black, naturally. Bastion reached around me to pull it out and slung it onto his shoulder. I guessed it made sense that he'd be prepared; he was an assassin and he probably lived his life out of that holdall. I didn't examine why I felt so begrudging that he was prepared, too.

Maxwell met us as we made our way in. The blond man is solidly ripped but his ever-present friendly smile always makes him feel less of a threat. No doubt that is his intention. His partner, Roscoe, is the head of The Pit; the fire elemental's ruling body. I liked Roscoe well enough but I liked Maxwell more; he always saved me a blueberry muffin on the days that I went in. It's the small things that count. It was late and I had no doubt that the blueberry muffins had long since been eaten, but I wouldn't hold it against him this time.

Rosie's had closed hours ago. As Maxwell shepherded me to the portal, I declined his polite offer of a cappuccino. I didn't want the caffeine jolt just before bed. The portal is housed in what appears to be a back room, discreetly marked with the symbol for the Other realm – three triangles inside each other surrounded by a circle. I opened the door, strolled in and immediately walked back out into the Common realm. Immediately the itching was gone.

Maxwell was still standing behind the counter but now the flames on his head had been replaced by a mop of stylish blond hair. My Other realm glasses had been removed, leaving me unable to see the magic that still existed around me. Maxwell was still in the Other realm with fire dancing on his head, but I couldn't see it no matter how hard I tried. Maxwell could shish-kebab me where I stood – he wouldn't, because that would be absurdly bad for business – and that vulnerability made me want to whimper. I despise the Common realm with its blue skies and green grass; give me the lilac skies of the Other, with its turquoise grass and black-barked trees. The Common realm's colour palette always seems so dull next to the psychedelic colours of the Other.

I had walked into the portal a witch and strolled out significantly less. My magic was still there but it was a tiny tendril compared to its usual torrent, barely enough to activate a rune. I hated the feeling of vulnerability and I toyed with the potion bomb in my skirt pocket. I had magic enough to light that if needed.

Oscar ducked in and out of the portal too. We were both ordinary now. Like me, Oscar is powerful enough to still access the tiniest amount of magic in the Common realm, but it wouldn't be enough to save us. The weakest witches and wizards lose all of their magic in the Common realm so I was grateful that I could still feel the hum of my magic inside me. I think I would have gone crazy without it.

Bastion remained where he stood, one eye on the exit and entrance. As a 'creature', he had no need to re-charge his batteries and he was ready to go all the time.

Lucky bastard. 'Miss DeLea is currently under threat,' he explained to Maxwell in a hard voice. 'I want your men on active standby.'

Maxwell nodded, straightened and looked at me far more seriously. 'You got it. You might be in the small room but it's no less secure.'

Bastion nodded his approval. 'Good. Show me.'

Maxwell ran through the security arrangements, including blast doors, metal shutters and five fire elementals on standby. Maxwell explained they would be on six-hour shifts.

'Make it four,' Bastion ordered. 'People get sloppy after that.' Maxwell promised to make changes to the roster.

Exhaustion was weighing down my limbs and sleep was crooning my name like the seductress she is. She was about the most action I'd had in years apart from my romance books. Jake hadn't been up for such things after his accident. It had been a long, cold, twenty years; there were probably cobwebs down there.

I cleared my throat impatiently and gave Bastion a pointed look. He turned to Maxwell. 'Sorry, she can't wait to get to bed.'

I felt myself flush. He was absolutely implying monkey business. Jerk. 'Can we move this along?' I huffed. 'I'm tired. It's been a long day. Which witch runed the room?'

'Say that five times fast!' Maxwell grinned before wiping the smile off his face at my chastening look. 'Erm, sorry. It was your lady, Meredith Plath, about two weeks ago. She's due for a rune check tomorrow, but they normally last at least four weeks.'

I nodded. Meredith was a powerful witch and I had no doubt that the runes would be fine. Nevertheless, I'd use what little magic I had to test them when we were safely inside.

Maxwell led us in and I did my best to hide my dismay. I rarely stay overnight at Rosie's these days, preferring the sanctuary of the coven tower, and I'd never stayed in this hovel. It was tiny! There was a small sofa on which Oscar would be hard pressed to fit, and a solitary bedroom. There was a bathroom and a kettle and a TV, and that was it. I was tempted to turn around and walk back out, but just the thought of that made my heavy limbs complain. What did it matter how poky the room was when I was only going to face plant on the bed?

'Thanks,' I muttered to Maxwell, managing to keep the sarcasm out of my voice with herculean effort. He left us to it and Bastion locked the heavy door behind him.

I touched the wall and summoned forward that tiny whisper of magic. It felt sluggish and slow to respond. I pulled harder and it answered, giving enough juice to light up the wards hidden on the walls. All but swaying on my feet, I studied them. Using this last bit of magic would send me over the edge and plunge me into full-on exhaustion, but the runes looked fine. I let the magic go with relief. We were safe.

'I'm going to sleep,' I announced. 'We can take turns on the bed, if you like,' I offered Oscar politely, knowing full well he wouldn't take me up on it.

'It's fine,' he assured me. 'I'll take the sofa. Sleep well, Am.'

'Good night, Oscar.' Carrying my go-bag, I went into the bedroom. I put it on the bed and rifled through it for my spare toiletry bag. As I turned to go to the bathroom, I stifled a scream as I almost walked into Bastion. 'What are you doing?' I asked him, my voice an octave higher than usual.

'Sleeping.'

'Out there!' I pointed back to the room where Oscar was.

'No. I'm not leaving you. Something still doesn't feel right.'

I blinked. 'There's only one bed!'

'It's a double,' he pointed out calmly.

I flushed. 'I'm not sharing a bed with you!'

'Typical only child,' he retorted.

I marched out, clutching my washbag and nightclothes. Oscar was already snoring on the sofa. I was incredibly jealous of his ability to fall asleep in a matter of minutes; I'd remarked on it before and all he'd said was 'military background', like that explained everything. More than once I'd demanded that he elaborate and each time he said, 'If I told you more I'd have to kill you.' He said it in all seriousness, so I'd eventually stopped asking. Whatever he'd done before joining the Coven was his business.

In the bathroom I changed into my pyjamas: silk shorts and a strappy top. I wished I'd brought something a little less revealing but it didn't matter; Bastion didn't care what I wore.

I strode back into the bedroom and faltered again. There was a chair that hadn't been there before and Bastion was sitting on it, long legs stretched out in front of him and crossed at the ankles. He passed me some pills. 'For your headache,' he murmured quietly.

'Thanks,' I mumbled. I hadn't once complained of a headache, so how did he know I was suffering? I decided that he must know the side effects of scrying. He was at least two hundred years old and he was bound to have picked up all sorts of information in that time.

'Goodnight, Amber.'

'Night,' I replied begrudgingly. Good manners don't cost anything, though at that moment I felt like a slice of pride was the price. The double bed looked spacious and empty and I felt like a dick.

I climbed in and snuggled into the sheets. I tried to sleep but, despite my exhaustion, I tossed and turned, my conscience prickling as Bastion sat on the uncomfortable wooden chair. I kept my eyes tightly closed as I finally said, 'Just get in the damned bed.'

He chuckled softly and I hated what a nice sound it was. 'Go to sleep, Amber.'

Ugh. I tried to shut off my mind but it kept recalling the long day we'd had. Assassination attempts, necromancers and kidnapping. What would tomorrow bring? Whatever it was, with Bastion by my side I feared tomorrow would be even longer. And then exhaustion dragged me under.

Chapter 15

My phone rang, jerking me from a deep sleep. I sat up and looked for it blearily. Where was I? Rosie's. I rubbed my eyes, trying to scrub sleep from them.

'Catch,' Bastion said.

I looked up in time to see my phone sailing towards me. I caught it clumsily; it would have been embarrassing if it had smacked me in the face. My phone told me it was 4.30am. Nothing good ever comes of answering the phone at 4.30am.

It was Jeb, the coven witch in charge of all things maintenance. Really? Could something being broken not wait until a more civilised hour – like 6am? I answered the phone. 'Morning, Jeb.' I skipped the 'good'. It wasn't a good morning if it started at 4.30am.

'Oh, thank fuck!' He expelled the words in a rush. 'She's okay!' he shouted, making me move the phone away from my ear.

'Who is okay?' I asked impatiently.

'You. Somebody bombed your flat.'

'Somebody bombed my flat?' I repeated dumbly. Bastion swore darkly. 'Is everyone okay?' I asked as my brain kicked in.

'Yes, fine. The bomb was highly contained due to your wards. The Symes attended promptly and sorted the fire. We're fine, but I promised Dick Symes another favour from you.'

I grimaced. I hoped Jeb had at least tried to curtail the extent of the favour because he was entirely too trusting at times. 'Where was the bomb planted?'

'Your bedroom.'

Grimmy. Shit. I hoped that the fireproof safe was bomb proof too. 'My office?'

'It's fine,' Jeb reassured me. 'It really was just your bedroom. When the bomb detonated it made quite a noise and we found the fire quickly.'

And I hadn't felt my wards being triggered because I was here in the Common realm. Dammit.

'Okay, I'm on my way.' I hung up. My research was hidden in the lab off my office and it was just my bedroom that was destroyed. That was good. I was lucky I was at Rosie's instead of at home. If I'd been home... I shuddered. Someone really did have me in their crosshairs.

Suddenly Bastion's presence in my life didn't seem such an imposition. I'd put up with the devil himself if he kept me alive.

I washed and dressed automatically then approached Oscar cautiously. 'Oscar,' I called his name softly before increasing my volume. On the third 'Oscar' he jerked awake and flung out his hands, ready to use the IR on me – but he didn't. Once, I'd made the mistake of shaking his shoulder to wake him and he'd thrown me against a wall. That had hurt like a bitch. Now I knew better. Never mind sleeping dragons – never wake a sleeping soldier.

Oscar woke sharp eyed and ready. 'There's been a bomb, we've got to go,' I explained.

'Where?' he asked, already pulling on his clothes.

'My bedroom,' I admitted.

Oscar stilled with one leg in his trousers. 'Fuck!' he swore.

'Mum would kick your behind for that.' We shared a quick look of regret that she wasn't here to do just that. Oscar carried on dressing then we gathered our stuff and headed out.

The door was being guarded by Maxwell himself, standing ready and alert. I was both surprised and gratified to see him; I would have expected him to be watching whoever was occupying the swish open-plan flat that the high-rollers paid for, not this dingy hovel I was in. 'Problem?' he asked as we walked out far earlier than we'd planned.

'There's been a bomb at the coven tower,' I admitted.

He whistled. 'Someone *has* got you on their shit-list.' He looked at Bastion with greater understanding. 'At least you've not got the griffins gunning for you too if Bastion's looking after you. That'd be a conflict of interest for the Guild.'

'Yes,' I muttered. 'I'm very lucky.' My sarcasm wasn't veiled.

'Do you want me to come with you?' Maxwell offered. 'I'm a bit of an expert on incendiary devices.'

I opened my mouth to deny him but Bastion nodded. 'Come with us,' he ordered. The man didn't know how to say please; I'd make it my life's work to teach him some damned manners.

Downstairs, Oscar and I trotted into and out of the portal. I managed to hold in my sigh of relief when my magic returned, now I was fully charged, able and willing, thank the Goddess. Despite the lack of sleep, I felt sharp and alert.

Someone really was trying to kill me – it wasn't something hypothetical anymore. First the vampyr, now this; someone had painted a target on my back. If they wanted to stop me from succeeding with my potion – well, they didn't know me at all. This was the added incentive I needed to boost the ORAL potion to the top of my to-do list. Once I created the potion, once it was out there in the world, there wouldn't be any point in killing me.

The coven tower was a hive of activity. The fire was out but the room was still smoking and it smelled acrid and threatening. A chill ran up my spine and I tried hard not to show how freaked out I was. Someone had planted a *bomb* in my room. And it had gone off successfully. This wasn't some half-assed amateur.

'Any idea what started it?' I asked Jeb briskly. 'We're definitely looking at an ordinary bomb versus anything magical, right?'

'We're not sure at this point,' Jeb admitted. 'Our focus was on getting the flames under control and minimising the damage. It's not as bad as it looks,' he tried to reassure me.

Good, because it looked Goddess-awful. 'The runes?'

Jeb grimaced. 'They were cancelled, Coven Mother. All of them.'

A witch, then; someone who had access to our tower, could light up the runes and scrawl *ezro* on them all. I had a black witch living under my very nose and now they were trying to *kill me.* It was hard not to take that personally.

Equally, there would be something personal about it when I hunted them down and threw them to the Connection for justice.

Chapter 16

Maxwell did his thing. It turned out the bomb had been placed under my bed. It was going to be quite some time before I slipped into bed without looking under it – not for monsters, but for explosives.

He found the remains of the incendiary device and pulled the scraps together. 'I'll take these home and analyse them then report back with my findings,' he promised.

'Appreciate that.' Bastion gave him a manly handshake and a clap on the arm. He approved of people who knew what they were doing, and Maxwell clearly did.

I chucked everyone out of the remains of my room. My clothes were gone – all I had left were the spares in my go-bag – but my anxiety was about the safe. Nobody knew about the existence of the safe bar the man who had installed it, so the black witch had no reason to put the bomb close to it, but the blackened remains of the cupboard door were making me nervous. If I was responsible for losing Grimmy after a dozen descendants before me had managed to keep him safe...

The cupboard door looked like a block of charcoal. I pulled it open and breathed a sigh of relief when I saw that the safe behind it looked undamaged. I reached out and promptly burnt myself on the metal. Ouch! Who'd have thought metal next to a huge fire would be searingly hot? Dammit, it was going to blister.

I wrapped some of my voluminous skirt around my hand, put in the code and yanked the handle. A back-up copy of my research sat safely ensconced next to Grimmy. I hauled Grimmy out. He looked okay. I stroked a finger down his spine and hoped we wouldn't need blood. The last thing I needed was to spill my blood on top of everything else.

Grimmy hovered upwards, flicking his pages open. 'Why, hello Miss Amber. What did you decide?'

'I'm working with the griffin,' I admitted.

'Marvellous, marvellous. I knew you had it in you to make the right choice. The DeLea name will be revered again.'

'It's already revered,' I groused. I worked my butt off to make sure of that.

Grimmy paused then he said, 'There seems to be some fire damage to your room, Miss Amber.'

'No? Really?'

'Sarcasm is the lowest form of wit,' he told me disapprovingly.

'Did you come up with that all by yourself?' I asked, my tone patronising.

If he'd been a real person rather than a book, I knew he'd be glaring at me. 'Are you quite done?' His pages ruffled.

'I'm not sure. Have I told you that sarcasm gives you the ability to insult stupid people without them realising it?' Was I implying Grimmy was stupid? Maybe. Was he happy about that? No.

He closed his pages and landed with a thump on the floor. Whoops. I'd pissed him off so much that he'd decided our conversation wasn't worth wasting life on. He wasn't wrong; with only so much time on this Earth, life is too short to waste time on things that don't make you happy. That was why my mother had taught me to care less about what others thought about me and more about what *I* thought about myself. Luckily, I think the world of myself.

There was a knock on my door. Bastion didn't wait for me to tell him to enter before plunging in. He looked around with a frown. 'I heard voices.'

I shrugged. He looked at the book on the blackened floor and my open safe door. 'The safe didn't get broken into?'

'No, it's all there.'

'So they didn't care about retrieving your research, only destroying it.'

'Destroying *me*,' I countered. 'If they had truly cared about ruining my research, both of my offices would have been destroyed.'

'You never stay overnight at Rosie's,' he said slowly.

'No, not usually.'

'What made you do it this time?'

I shrugged again. 'I was tired.' It seemed ridiculous, but being exhausted had saved my life. The Goddess had guided me.

Bastion continued, 'The thing with the kid was a ploy.'

I frowned. 'To do what?'

'To draw you away. They knew Ada would summon you to look for the kid so you'd be out of the tower. They planted the bomb while you were guaranteed to be away from home.'

'I could have delegated it, though. I wanted to. And how could they know when I'd arrive at Ada's?'

'They had access to the roster and they knew no one else would be available. And they had a watcher. At least,

I would have had one if it'd been me. Someone who messaged them when you arrived at the Marlow place. Then the black witch went into your home, cancelled all your runes, planted the bomb, set the timer and waited for you to die.'

The last words made me swallow and I looked away so he wouldn't see how freaked out I was. Definitely an insider job, then. This was a nightmare.

When I looked back, he was studying me and I hated that he probably wasn't fooled in the slightest. I was feeling vulnerable and raw, and he was feeling bad for me. I didn't want – or deserve – anyone's pity. 'My romance books are all gone,' I said to change the subject. I waited for him to say something scathing about my reading tastes.

His dark eyes met my green ones and I couldn't tell what he was thinking. 'You'll have to start a new collection,' he said finally.

I swallowed the lump in my throat. It was absurd to be upset about losing my book collection. I was *alive* and I should be grateful. But reading was one of the few things that I did for *me,* and my romance books had kept me going through some very lonely moments.

I cleared my throat to make sure my voice didn't warble when I spoke. 'Where is everyone?' The room outside had fallen silent.

'Maxwell has taken the bomb shards and left. Jeb has measured up everything that needs to be replaced. Ethan has repainted all the runes on your walls. Oscar has gone to check your office downstairs.'

'They're all gone.'

'Yes. Except for me.'

I sighed a little. 'You're always here.'

'Like glue.'

'I don't often have glue on me,' I responded drily.

'You should remedy that. Glue is always useful.' I wasn't sure if we were still talking about glue. 'What do you want to do now?' he asked.

'Cry?' The answer slipped out before my brain connected with my mouth. I hastily waved the comment away lest he take me seriously. I couldn't go around letting people see I had feelings – good Goddess, what would Mum say? I walked into my living room, mostly to walk away from my comment which was entirely too honest to share with Bastion.

The living room looked normal, a little mucky from all the people tramping in and out of my ash-covered bedroom, but apart from that an oasis of calm. I looked out of my window and smiled as I spotted the familiar black raven hovering outside. I opened the window. 'Hey,

Fehu,' I called to him. He flew in and landed on my shoulder.

'Fehu?' Bastion said, amused.

Fehu turned his head to studiously ignore Bastion, making me smile. 'It's the rune for luck,' I said a shade defensively. 'He flew to me once when he had broken wings. He shouldn't have been able to make it that far.'

Bastion froze and his nostrils flared. 'Did he now?' His voice had gone glacially cold. 'Who would harm a bird?'

I blinked then understood: of course he was outraged, he was part-bird himself.

Bastion studied the raven and then studied me. 'You healed him?' He asked the question like he already knew the answer.

I folded my arms. 'Of course I healed him.'

He was still looking at me like I was a puzzle he couldn't solve. 'He can't pay you,' he said finally.

'Obviously not,' I glared. 'There's more to life than money.'

'I know that.' He looked surprised. 'But I didn't know that *you* did.'

I ignored the sting of hurt his words caused. Of course there was more to life than money but money sure helped make life easier. It got my mum her treatment and her care;

it bought me ingredients to make life-saving potions. For good or ill, money wasn't without value.

I went to the fridge and found some ham for Fehu. He happily hopped from foot to foot as I fed him. 'He seems to like you,' Bastion said, amused.

'Or my ham,' I countered. I bit my lip. 'He's only been around a few weeks. Should I be worried about his motivation?' My gut said he was fine, but that seemed a bit wishy-washy now that my bedroom had been blown up.

Bastion gave a low kraa and Fehu flew from my hand to his outstretched one. He studied the bird. 'His intentions are pure,' he said finally. 'He likes you and wants to help you.'

'How can you tell?'

'I'm a coaxer,' he pointed out. 'I can't induce him to hurt you. He's not here for anything nefarious. He likes you, your pretty hair and your ham.'

I touched a hand self-consciously to my red locks. 'Not everyone likes a ginger.'

'It's a warning that you're too hot to handle. Not everyone can deal with the heat. Don't take it personally. Only a real man can handle a redhead.'

Embarrassingly, I felt myself blush. That was the nicest thing anyone had ever said about my redheaded charms. I'd been tempted in my teen years to dye my hair but Mum had threatened to cut it all off if I did. The urge hadn't arisen again; I accepted my looks now. I was me: take it or leave it.

Bastion lifted his hand and Fehu flew from his fingers, circling the room once before leaving through the window. He'd checked on me, had his ham and departed. Fair enough.

'It's still early,' Bastion noted. 'What are your plans for today?'

'Potion making.' My tone was grim. The faster I made this damned potion, the faster I got my life back.

Chapter 17

I enjoyed my morning with my cauldrons; nothing calms the mind like routine work. I wanted to make more of the base that I'd ended up using to help the vampyrs instead of using in my ORAL potion. The next stage would be tricky, mostly because the ingredients were difficult to get – read 'impossible'. But the clue was in the name: 'I'm possible'; it was only a failure when you gave up.

There had been banging and clattering for the past hour and Bastion had ducked out to check on the ruckus. 'Jeb,' he'd explained on his return, like that was sufficient explanation. It probably was: Jeb was busy doing what was necessary to make my room habitable again and I appreciated the effort. I'd probably need to get out a blow-up bed for tonight, but hopefully we could get the flooring sorted and the walls re-plastered in short order. We keep a bunch of tradesmen on retainer and I'm happy to pay a steep premium to be bumped up to the top of their lists.

When the potion base was stable, I turned off the flames and stirred it until it cooled, then I covered the cauldrons and painted fresh *isa* runes on both of them. The stasis rune would keep them in good actionable condition. Technically I had plenty of time to get the next ingredients, but really I had no time to waste while someone was hunting me as if I were their next meal.

I sent a coven-wide email summoning everyone available to the common room immediately. I gave it ten minutes before I went down with Bastion on my heels. There was a chorus of 'Coven Mother!' as I walked in. Venice was giving happy sobs at the sight of me, which was nice if overdone. Everyone looked happy to see me, even Sarah, Venice's daughter, who'd been bumped back down to acolyte.

I suffered through a fair amount of hugging and pats on my shoulder that I endured because they needed to reassure themselves that I was still alive after the bomb. Hannah gave me a tearful handshake, which felt weird, but I think she was just trying to respect my boundaries. Tenby gave me a nod. They looked to be getting on well, which was good – but not too well, which was also good.

John, the Spice Shoppe's owner, either didn't know about my boundaries or didn't respect them because he pulled me into a bear-hug. 'We'll get them,' he said, outraged. 'This cannot be allowed to stand!' There was fury on every line of his face – and his wasn't the only one. My coven was riled. I was quietly pleased; it was more than a little gratifying to know how much people seemed to care that someone was trying to kill me.

After everyone had spoken to me, I went to the centre of the room and held up my hand for silence. It fell instantly. 'Thank you all for your concern for my well-being. As you no doubt know by now, a bomb was placed in my bedroom.' Shocked gasps echoed around the room. Hmm, maybe not everyone had known that.

'I am fine, despite someone's nefarious intentions. I have gathered you all here to bring something very serious to your attention.'

Ria and her mum Meredith sidled in. I motioned for them to sit and carried on with my speech. 'The only way someone could have planted a bomb in my room is by deactivating the runes on my walls. It saddens me to say this, but I have seen additional evidence that we have a black witch practising amongst us.'

Someone wailed; my money was on Sarah because she loved a drama. I shot a look at Venice, but she was looking aghast. I scanned the crowd to see if there was anyone who did not look shocked or horrified. Ethan, next to his partner Jacob, looked grim. Jeb's fists were clenched in rage and he was looking around as if he could tell who the traitor was just by looking at them. Much like I was.

Meredith had paled and her hands were covering her mouth as if she were going to be sick. She was clutching Ria's hands as her familiar, a cat named Cindy, coiled around her legs giving her comfort with a soft *mrrow*. Cindy was a coven fixture; she was social and affectionate and was often found in the common room. When no one was around, I stroked her and her warm affection always made me feel better. I envied Meredith that comfort now.

Henry was standing next to Ria, trying to get her attention rather than gasping with everyone else. Nobody looked guilty except perhaps Briony Fields, though I suspected that guilt was her default expression. She was normally guilty of something; usually bone idleness. She never did a jot more than was required and sometimes significantly less. Still, her lazy work ethic could be a smokescreen; she was so lazy that she was rarely asked to do jobs because you couldn't trust her to do them properly. That meant she had plenty of time for black witchery. Plus, the black witch's rune on Frankie had been sloppy and so had the grasp on the vampyrs. I bumped her up the suspect list.

'Keep your eyes peeled. Keep your noses clean. Report anything weird. Dismissed,' I snapped. I met Oscar's eyes and gave him a nod, asking him to stay and keep his ear to the ground. He gave a faint nod in response, then struck up a conversation with John Melton. Hug or not, John would have access to plenty of ingredients for darker potions. He was on the list, too.

I walked out, leaving my coven gossiping amongst themselves. 'Was that wise?' Bastion spoke up as we returned to my flat. 'Now the black witch knows that you're onto them.'

'This whole thing reeks of an insider job. Only an idiot would think it was anything else. Ergo, black witch. I would prefer people were alert and on guard.'

'You're going to start a witch-hunt.' His tone was grim.

I sighed. 'I know.' It wasn't ideal but I wouldn't be able to sleep at night if I didn't say something and warn them. What if I wasn't the only target of the black witch? No, better that they were on their guard.

I wished again that Jinx wasn't on her honeymoon. She is a truth-seeker and she can tell every time you lie, though that isn't widely known. All I would need to do was parade my coven in front of her and she'd weed out the black witch faster than you could say 'rotten egg'.

The thing is, I'm a great leader. I'm organised, I work hard, I try and recognise people's skills and talents – but I am not a detective. I don't know the first thing about finding people. Luckily, I had a murderous griffin following me around who happened to be the best tracker on the planet. He had to be able to find this witch, and hopefully he could do it before he or she succeeded in bombing me to smithereens.

I hated to ask for help, especially from him, but I'd do just about anything for the good of my coven – including swallowing my pride. I hoped that I wouldn't choke on it.

Chapter 18

Oscar called me. 'There's someone in your office downstairs to see you.'

'Who?'

He hesitated. 'The temporary coven mother has arrived.'

'Who?' I repeated more insistently.

'In life, there are some things you have to find out for yourself.' He hung up. Coward.

I glared at the phone. I could only think of one person with whom I'd be really pissed off at handing over the reins. Ultimately, I just didn't have the time to do everything that I needed to. I'd been working in my private office for three hours already, hammering out schedules, checking potions supplies and invoices and checking the coven's coffers. It was all absolutely necessary but time consuming. Not to mention all the teaching I'd scheduled for the coming week, including complex rune spreads and potion interactions. I love teaching, but right now it was just another thing that was keeping me away from my potion breakthrough.

I strode down the stairs to my coven office, trying not to mutter audibly as I went. Only crazy people talk to themselves. Bastion followed me, silent as ever.

I marched into my office and froze. Kassandra Scholes. Of course it was. Of all the people they had to send to take over, it had to be her. She smiled at me, her long brown hair no doubt hiding her little lizard familiar that always skittered around her neck. I swear, she does it on purpose. I don't like lizards, so naturally that's what Kassandra's familiar is – a lizard. Ugh.

She was sitting in *my* chair. 'Who is running your coven while you're here?' I finally asked, when I could be sure I had a civilised tongue in my mouth.

'My second in command, Stevie,' Kassandra replied lightly. I didn't have a second in command; there was Ethan, maybe even Jeb, but neither of them could run the whole tower without me. Oscar would have been my preference, but some people took issue with him being a wizard rather than a witch. And anyway, I have real issues with delegation. Why give a job to someone else when I can do it better, faster?

Next to Kassandra was another witch, one I didn't recognise. 'Who is this?'

'My assistant, Becky Chose.'

I resisted the urge to ask what exactly Becky chose but didn't as I had no doubt that I wasn't being as witty as I thought I was. 'You're in my chair,' I pointed out.

'I rather thought that was the point of all of this,' Kassandra noted drily. 'Why do you have a pet griffin?'

Bastion let out a noise that could only be described as a growl and Kassandra flinched. 'No disrespect to you, of course,' she added hastily.

'Just to Miss DeLea,' he said darkly.

Kassandra blinked. 'We have a banterous relationship.'

'We have a relationship?' I asked in surprise.

'A banterous one,' Kassandra confirmed.

'I thought we were rivals.'

'That, too. And yet here I sit, invited to coven-sit for you while you do something big and important. The coven council wouldn't tell me what it is but, even so, I'm here to assist you. Truly.'

I studied her and found to my surprise that I believed her. She was here to help. 'This is bigger than either of us,' I said finally. 'It is important.' I didn't want to hint about my project because it would be just my luck to have Kassandra decide to take an interest in it and badda-bing, badda-boom she'd create the same potion a day earlier than me, pulling the rug out from under my feet. Like me, she is annoyingly good at potion creation.

The smile dropped from her face and she nodded. 'I know. Whatever you're doing, it's for the good of witches everywhere.'

I raised a cynical eyebrow. 'And if it means I secure the position as the Symposium member?'

'Then the best witch has won.' She shrugged then leaned forward in *my* chair. 'I have no doubt that this is a test for us both. Can we work together? Can we set aside our personal differences for the good of the coven? Because I can and I will.'

I nodded once. 'Fine.'

'Fine.'

I gestured to the computer in front of her. 'I've been working on rotas and fund allocation this morning. I have teaching in my diary across the next week.'

'I'll take over those obligations for you,' Kassandra confirmed evenly.

'I'll let it be known that you're acting as temporary Coven Mother. I keep an open-door policy. I expect you to do the same.'

Her assistant Becky harrumphed, eyes narrowed at me in obvious dislike. 'Kassandra always has an open-door policy. She's an exemplary Coven Mother.'

'Becky,' Kassandra chastened. 'I don't need you to fight my battles for me.'

'No, Coven Mother.' Becky subsided, but she still shot me an extra glare when Kassandra wasn't looking. She had a pad in her hand and was making notes. I had no idea exactly what she was noting, but it was probably *Amber is a bitch*.

I wanted to show Becky who was boss but technically Kassandra was still her boss, even if they were on my territory. Some days, it felt like my greatest accomplishment was keeping my mouth shut. 'I'll let you settle in then.' I stood.

'We arrived yesterday,' Becky muttered petulantly. 'We've settled just fine.'

'I met with friends for dinner,' Kassandra explained. 'I hope the delay wasn't an issue.' She wasn't exactly apologising for dragging her heels but I shrugged it off – that, and the jealousy that she had friends to have dinner with.

'Not at all,' I said coolly. 'In any case, I had several matters yesterday that I preferred to have dealt with personally.' I doubted Ada Marlow would have accepted

Kassandra in my place, though I wondered if the bomb would have been under Kass's pillow if she had. Was someone targeting me or just any old witch? I grimaced. I needed to be honest with myself. It was me, definitely me. I needed to be alert and take this risk seriously.

I had my tote bag full of potions and brushes so I went back to the coven common room where I found Oscar sitting with Henry and Ethan. Henry is Ethan's son but he manages to be far more personable then his father – Jacob's influence, no doubt. The common room was still full and buzzing with people.

Oscar rose as I approached and took out his car keys. I held up one finger to signal for him to give me a minute.

I cleared my throat. 'Attention please.' Silence fell gratifyingly quickly. 'I have a brief announcement to make. Due to other commitments, I am temporarily seconding my title as Coven Mother to Kassandra Scholes. She will be here, with her assistant Becky, until such a time as my other project is concluded. Please welcome them both. That will be all.'

Whispers broke out. I heard Sarah say to Ria, 'I bet her project is hunting the black witch!'

At least that gave me a handy cover for what I was really doing. The fewer people who knew about my potion the better. Let them think that I was donning Sherlock

Holmes' deerstalker; better that than them knowing the truth.

Business concluded, I found Oscar's eyes in the crowd and jerked my head to the door. He stood again and we made our way to the garage. We got in the car, with Bastion ever present.

It was flirting with evening and I'd been so busy getting my affairs in order that I'd only had a measly sandwich for lunch. My stomach growled but I ignored it. The hunger would fade when I got stuck into work. I didn't need to tell Oscar where we were going because he knew my diary better than I did.

He drove us to a clinic in Slough. A poem was written about Slough in the 1930s when industry had taken hold of the town. The poem called for bombs to fall on it, which was a bit extreme by any standard. It isn't *that* bad, though it is still a deprived area, which is why the pop-up clinic is located there.

I took over the GP practice once a week, twice when my schedule allowed it, and I'd had people come from as far as Birmingham to see me. Giving away healing for free is frowned on almost as much as not having a familiar, so I took steps to ensure my anonymity by donning my cloak and lifting the cowl to hide my face. I'd bought the cloak especially from the seers; seer-spelled objects are pricey but worth it. The bespelled cowl cloaked my face in shadows, hiding my red hair and green eyes.

The reception area was full and noisy; it would be a long evening. I was late, only by five minutes but it wasn't an auspicious start to my appointments. The people waiting fell silent as they caught sight of Bastion. I cleared my throat. 'It's fine,' I assured them. 'He's just a friend. He's helping me tonight.' The wary silence remained.

'Good evening, Ellie,' Janice on reception greeted me, trying to direct attention away from us.

'Good evening, Janice,' I replied. 'Give me two minutes, then send the first one in.'

Kassandra would take over some things, but not this. The clinic is my baby, my very-secret baby. That's why I use another name, Ellie Tron; in Greek, amber used to be called *elektron*. I'd thought I'd been so witty when I'd chosen that name for my clinic work. With hindsight, it wasn't so subtle; I would have been better calling myself Jane Doe.

I bustled into the office and pulled the supplies from my tote bag. As always, Bastion was a silent, brooding shadow, observing the room and me and missing nothing. I wondered if he'd pieced together why we were here; he wasn't stupid and he'd soon realise if he hadn't already.

He took up position, surreptitiously drawing the blinds on the window. The darkness made me glare at him, so he flipped on the light and its harsh brilliance filled the space. Too much light for my taste, but better than too little; he was banishing the shadows through which a vampyr could phase. I thought about telling him that there were anti-vampyr runes painted on the walls and there was another room where I saw vampyr clients if I needed to, but dismissed the idea. Better that he stay alert; vampyrs aren't the only ones that go bump in the night.

First on my clinic schedule was an imp. Janice knocked once before opening the door for the small creature. He was no bigger than the size of my hand and he was clutching a stump of a tail. He'd put a bandage around it to stop the bleeding, but he looked utterly miserable. 'Come on in,' I said gently to the forlorn creature.

He entered and Janice quietly closed the door behind him. Imps as a species are usually full of a mischievous energy that this one was definitely lacking. 'You're here for your tail?' Obviously he was, but I've found it is best to let people tell you a little about their problems.

He nodded. 'It got chopped off by a vampyr. He enchanted me so I couldn't move, then he said he was going to eat it!' His voice was shrill with outrage. 'He laughed. The bastard.'

Imps use their long tails rather like monkeys, wrapping them around objects and using them as ropes to haul themselves upwards. Without his tail, this imp's movements were sorely restricted.

Outrage stirred in my chest. Imps need their tails to move around, and the bastard vampyr thought he was giving his victim a long, slow, painful death. It is rare for me to swear, even within the confines of my own mind, but that vampyr was an asshole.

'Can you get up onto the table or shall I help you?' I kept all sympathy out of my voice, knowing he wouldn't welcome it.

'I got no money,' he stated pugnaciously, lifting his chin.

'The clinic is free,' I returned levelly. 'Shall I assist you?'

'Yeah, go on. I'd like a ride on you.' He gave me an exaggerated leer that I knew was largely to compensate for how uncomfortable he was feeling. I put my hand down to the ground and let him climb onto it before I lifted him slowly and carefully to table height. When I flattened my hand, the red-skinned imp walked off it.

His antlers were in fine condition – often the main reason imps come to me is an antler issue – but his tail was ragged and ruined. I carefully removed his makeshift bandage but he still cried out as I pulled away the fabric that was sticking to the gunky wound. Unless I could grow him a new tail he would die; without his tail to whip him out of trouble somebody would stand on him or drive over him.

'Can you fix it, witch?' His voice low but I heard the thread of hope in it.

'I can,' I said confidently and the little imp's eyes welled with tears. I gave him a moment and busied myself pulling out potions and brushes and pulling on my re-useable gloves. Finally I said, 'I'd like to take a picture of the injury, if I may.'

He nodded and I clicked one quickly on my phone.

The imp was dressed in a loincloth with the rest of his red skin bare. He was so small that I had very little skin on which to fit a lot of runes. I selected my tiniest brush. 'I'll need you to lie here and stay still,' I told him. He lay down and I pulled over a mounted magnifying glass. The lights were on full power but I also pulled over the desk light so I could see exactly what I was doing.

What followed was some of my finest-ever rune work. Once I had double-checked all sixteen of them, I pulled my magic forward. 'This will be uncomfortable,' I warned him.

I gave him a moment to brace himself, then directed my magic to the runes and breathed the word *isa* gently to activate them. *Isa* can be used to activate runes or to hold things in stasis; all runes have multiple meanings and uses, which is why their use and interactions aren't simple. It had taken years for me to become a rune master but now I am confident I am one of the best in the UK, if not the world.

The imp cried out as the runes lit up. I watched, eyes fixed on his tail, and the tension dropped from my shoulders as I saw it starting to grow. Thank the Goddess.

It wasn't a quick process – it took a further ten minutes before his new tail had grown right to its forked end. The imp sobbed helplessly when the fork reappeared and my eyes prickled. I occupied myself cleaning my brushes so he wouldn't see my unprofessional display of emotion.

Finally, the light faded from the runes and they disappeared from his body as if they'd never been there. 'One last thing, if I may?' I asked calmly.

'Anything, lady! Anything!' He clutched his tail to his chest, beaming.

'I want to scry the vampyr from your mind. It will leave you with a headache for a day or so – and one that magic can't get rid of – but I'll see justice done. Do you agree?'

'Yeah, do it, lady. Get that bitey fucker for me,' he said fiercely.

I poured some water into a bowl and painted a tiny rune on his head. 'This will hurt,' I warned again. 'Picture the vampyr that did this to you then touch the water's surface.'

He did so and the snarling face of a vampyr filled the bowl. It was not one that I recognised but that was Wokeshire's issue, not mine. I took a picture of the image on my phone and texted it to Wokeshire, outlining the imp's accusations and sending a picture of the stump.

I gently cancelled the scry. The imp gasped and held a hand to his head. 'You weren't kidding. My head is pounding.'

'Sorry.' I winced in sympathy. 'Here, you can have some Common realm medicine.' I reached into the desk and pulled out a dissolvable painkiller. I broke it in half and then half again before adding it to a small amount of water. 'Drink this, it will help.'

He downed the fizzy mixture gratefully, making a face at the taste. 'It's worth the headache if you get the bastard,' he muttered, using his tail to climb rapidly up to my shoulder. By the time he arrived there he was smiling again, filled with the joy of using his tail.

With a suspicious glance at Bastion, he leaned in and whispered quietly into my ear, 'If you need help escaping the griffin, just cough and I'll cause a distraction.'

My heart warmed. 'I'm fine, thank you,' I promised. 'He's looking after me.'

'Is he? That's good.' The imp leaned closer and pressed a soft kiss to my cheek. 'Witch known as Ellie, I can't see your face but I give you my kiss. If ever you have need of me, press your fingers to it and I'll come to you. You may call me Frogmatch.'

'Two rules. No names and the clinic is free,' I repeated firmly. 'You do not need to give me anything, even your name.'

'Perhaps not, but I *want* to give it. It is my gift to you, so mote it be,' Frogmatch said firmly.

'So mote it be,' I agreed softly. The imp grinned at me before swinging down and letting out a triumphant yowl as he ran under the door, out of the room and away.

The intercom buzzed. 'Next?' Janice asked.

'Next,' I agreed.

Chapter 19

I worked until the clinic was empty. Some of the patients had been waiting nearly a week to see me and I hated that I hadn't been able to devote much time to the place during recent weeks. My research took precedence, though it would be worth it. I hoped I wasn't lying to myself because these patients needed me.

I packed up the remains of the potion pots. The evening had been heavy going, and my right hand was cramping in protest. I am fairly ambidextrous, but not sufficiently confident to risk using my left hand for intricate healing runes.

I'd let Janice go after she'd let in the last patient, so I did a quick walk through and locked the building. I checked the time: 1am. Ouch.

Bastion's voice made me jump. 'What is more pressing, your need for food or your pain?'

I scowled. 'I'm not in pain.'

'Your hand has been cramping for the last half an hour,' he noted with a faint frown.

I waved it away. 'It's fine. It happens. Food. Oscar will have something for us.' Sure enough, when we slid into the warmth of the car, we were greeted by the smell of food. 'Rice box?' I asked happily.

'Your favourite,' Oscar confirmed.

Yum. He passed me the little cardboard carton crammed to the brim with chicken fried rice and I dived in, noticing that Bastion was doing the same. I felt a twinge of guilt. It was all well and good for me to go without food when I was busy, but I shouldn't make him do the same. He probably needed a zillion calories a day.

A thought occurred to me. 'Um,' I said after my mouth was empty, 'how are you on the killing front?'

Bastion looked amused. 'Are you concerned?'

'No! But if you do need to go hunting, I have a vampyr that's pissed me off,' I half-joked.

'I'm good. I'm more than two hundred years old, so I have my urges under control.'

'Okay. Well, tell me if that changes,' I ordered. The last thing I needed was an out-of-control griffin on my hands.

'Do you want me to kill the vampyr for you?' he asked, as if he were asking if I needed a loaf of bread from the shops.

'No, thank you. Wokeshire will deal with him,' I said confidently. Silence fell and Bastion and I fell on our rice pots again as Oscar drove us back to the coven tower.

'Have you got a spare blow-up bed?' I asked Oscar after we parked up. I should have checked sooner. My bedroom was destroyed; there is a penthouse flat that we keep free for emergencies and prestigious visitors, but now it was housing Kassandra and probably her assistant. Besides, I wanted my home, partly because of its comforts and partly to show my attackers I wasn't cowed. Screw you if you think you'll drive me away.

'You won't need one,' Oscar assured me. 'Jeb was outraged. He's called in favours left, right and centre for you.'

'But surely my bedroom can't be habitable?' I said dubiously.

'See for yourself.'

We climbed the stairs, even though I wanted to be lazy and grab the lift. Oscar said goodnight when we reached his floor and pulled me in for a rare hug. 'Sleep well, Am.' He pressed a kiss to my forehead; the attack on me had shaken him more than he was letting on.

I hugged him back; it had shaken me, too. 'You too.'

Bastion and I kept climbing until we reached my flat. The nine on the door had swung down to the six position but that wasn't surprising with everyone and his dog tramping through to get the place fixed. Maybe Bastion was right; maybe my six/nine system wasn't all that effective, and we'd already learned that runes could be bypassed if you knew a black witch talented enough to do it.

When I stepped into my bedroom, I gasped. There was a huge king-size bed, larger than my previous double, surrounded by fitted wardrobes. The bed was a four poster raised on wooden legs. It looked good – though I couldn't help remembering that the bomb had been planted under my last bed and this one, on stilts, was virtually begging for another one.

The charred carpet was gone, replaced by wooden flooring and a plush rug. Someone had dressed the room with maroon accents – curtains and cushions and the bedspread. It was beautiful. There was still a smell from the magnolia paint that had been splashed on the walls, but I had a room where this morning I'd only had a scorched mess.

There was a rock in my throat. Jeb deserved a pay rise. How he'd done this in such a short space of time, even with magic, was truly impressive. I flicked on a lamp experimentally and sure enough it lit up. He'd even managed to sort the electrics.

'He likes you,' Bastion commented.

'What?'

'Jeb.'

'He's a team player.'

Bastion shook his head, like I wasn't getting his point.

'Do you want a cup of tea before bed?' I asked. I needed one; it had been a long, stressful day and I needed to calm my nerves with a brew.

'Yes,' Bastion responded.

I occupied myself making tea. With a smirk that no one could see, I grabbed a mug for Bastion that said: *I've washed my fanny in this mug*. I'd started collecting mugs with witty or sarcastic comments on them when I was a teenager. This was a gag gift from Aunt Abigay that had made my mum snort tea out of her nose. Repugnant as the concept was, I'd never managed to throw it away though the thought of drinking from it was mildly abhorrent so it hadn't been used in years. I washed off the dust and selected a mug for myself that said: *Another fine day ruined by responsibility*. That mug wasn't wrong.

'Milk? Sugar?' I asked Bastion. I'd made him a cup of tea before, but I hadn't cared enough to ask about his preferences. Not that I cared now, but it was polite to ask.

'A little milk, not a lot. No sugar.'

I resisted the urge to dump in half a pint of milk because nobody likes a Petty Crocker. And suddenly Jake flickered into my mind; chucking me that roguish smile as he told me he wasn't 'sweet enough already' and piling heaps of sugar into his mug. Goddess damn. Even the simplest activity could make me think of him.

Tears welled and I struggled for a moment before I pushed aside the sharp shards of grief and focused on my task. When I was sure of my composure, I carried the brews over to where Bastion was sitting, his long legs stretched out under my coffee table.

He grinned as he read his mug. 'Impressive flexibility,' he joked, taking a sip.

Darn. I'd expected the mug to evoke a glare, not a smile; I hadn't expected him to have a sense of humour. 'Did you order extra security for my flat?' I asked to fill the silence.

Bastion grimaced. 'Yes, I have a man coming to fit the system tomorrow. A day too late.'

'We're not dead, so tomorrow is fine.' I shrugged and sipped my hot tea. If it wasn't scalding then where was the challenge?

'The clinic...' He trailed off.

'What about it?'

'You help all of those people for free?'

'Not everyone can afford to pay,' I said sharply. 'The exorbitant prices I charge the rest of the time cover the costs of running it.'

He nodded but he was looking at me strangely and it made me uncomfortable. I cast about for something else to say but I had nothing. We finished our brews in silence, but this time it felt more companionable.

I washed up both cups and went into my bathroom to brush my teeth and change into my nightclothes. When I walked out, Bastion was waiting. 'You're sleeping in my bedroom, I suppose?' I asked, resignedly.

'The bed is big enough,' he pointed out.

I nodded. Frankly, I didn't want him on my sofa; if another attack happened, I wanted him by my side.

He disappeared into the bathroom with his holdall and came padding out dressed in tiny boxer shorts. My mouth dropped open. No one had a right to have that many muscles – he even had a little V pointing towards his man-meat. I wondered how often he worked out because I hadn't seen him do so much as a single push-up since he'd started guarding me. Maybe it was just his natural physique.

I realised I was ogling and my cheeks heated. He might be easy on the eyes but it changed nothing between us. There was nothing between us to change.

I climbed into my bed, snuggled into the sheets and tried my best to forget that only the night before someone had planted a bomb under my bed, but 2am came around and I was still tossing and turning. I was exhausted but I couldn't shake my anxiety enough to relax into sleep.

Bastion gave a barely audible sigh, sat up next to me, grabbed his pillow and slid out of the bed. He threw the pillow under the bed and rolled under with it to lie on the hard wooden floor. 'What are you doing?' I asked, my voice a little shrill.

'I'm sleeping under your bed,' he explained evenly. There was no irritation in his tone.

'Why?' I asked blankly.

'Because then you'll know there's no bomb there. Go to sleep, Amber.'

I closed my eyes. I couldn't imagine anyone else that I knew sleeping under my bed to make me feel better; I wasn't a child, to be reassured that there were no monsters lurking there. It was getting harder and harder to cling to my narrative that Bastion was evil when he was being so blatantly nice. Not long ago, I would have counted him amongst the monsters but now I wasn't so sure.

Sleep claimed me in moments.

Chapter 20

'Cup of tea?' I asked.

Bastion nodded, not even complaining at the early hour despite our late night. I put enough water in for us both and switched on the kettle. As my pseudo-father Oscar likes to take care of me, in my fridge were two glasses of freshly squeezed orange juice and two bowls of oats that had been soaked overnight. I guessed he was taking care of Bastion now, too.

I put the drinks on the table, my tea milky and his darker. I gave him one of my favourite mugs, which said: *No fox given!* with a picture of a fox on it. Mine said: *I'm fine, everything is fine* and had a picture of an electrified cat. I wasn't fine but I was damned good at pretending I was.

Today I was on a mission to get stuff done – my ORAL potion, in particular. I'd been putting off harvesting some of the ingredients because it was dangerous, but now I had a live-in protector there would never be a safer time to go gathering.

I rang Tom Smith, one of the brethren and the dragon king's second in command. Even though Emory was on holiday, I knew he wouldn't mind me borrowing his stuff. For an only child, Emory is really good at sharing. 'Smith,' Tom answered gruffly.

'Tom, it's Amber DeLea.'

'Miss DeLea, what can I do for you?'

'I could do with a helicopter,' I admitted. Emory kept one – and a pilot – on retainer.

There were some clacking noises as Tom checked something on his computer. 'Chris is free. Where do you want to fly to?' It was gratifying that he didn't question whether or not Emory would lend me his helicopter and pilot.

'Scotland. Falkirk.'

'Okay, we'll need to check re-fuelling. You'll be pushing it from your place to Scotland – that will be just over two hours' flight time. Let me sort a refuel at Carlisle. Chris will be with you in half an hour. Make sure the helipad is clear.'

'Will do,' I hung up.

Bastion was studying me. 'I don't need a refuel. *I* could have flown you.'

I balked; trust issues aside, that was a *long* way to ride astride a giant flying lion. 'I've ridden on Shirdal a time or two and a quick five-minute ride is okay, but two or three hours would be a bit much. Plus a helicopter is much faster.' And comfier.

'You've ridden on Shirdal?'

'Yeah. So?'

His expression darkened and I felt like I'd stepped into a minefield though I didn't know why. To give myself a reason to turn away from his scowl, I dialled Jeb. 'Morning Amber,' he answered, yawning.

Oh heck, it was early. Really early. 'Sorry to wake you. I just wanted to check that the helipad was clear.' I should have just gone and looked rather than waking Jeb at the crack of dawn, but in for a penny in for a pound.

'It's all clear, Coven Mother,' he promised. He was waking up and the respectful title was back.

'Thank you.' I hung up, resisting the urge to apologise. Coven Mothers aren't supposed to apologise, we are supposed to demand and command. It literally says that in the handbook.

I went to my new wardrobe, expecting it to be empty after the fire had destroyed all my clothes, but there were about thirty things hanging there still with shopping tags attached. Tears sprang to my eyes; someone had cared enough to go shopping for me – Venice, perhaps, or Melrose. They were the main clotheshorses in the coven. Whoever it was, I was incredibly grateful. They'd got my usual full-length skirts in an array of colours, and a bunch of peasant-style blouses, all in my size. They hadn't bought the leggings that I usually wore underneath the skirts, but they weren't common knowledge.

Kindness always surprises me and I struggled to pull myself together. Finally I got my emotions – and my face – under control and prepared for a day of potion-ingredient collection. I painted on some protective runes before I dressed. I could have done with some leggings, but it couldn't be helped; the helicopter would be here soon and I didn't want to wait until the shops opened for the day.

I spoke my affirmations into my handheld mirror. 'It doesn't matter that you don't have a familiar. You are a strong successful witch. You don't need anyone or anything.' I gave myself a brisk nod. 'Today you are going to get some ingredients and be one step closer to success.' I set my mirror down and squared my shoulders.

Bastion had gotten our overnight oats out of the fridge. I struggle to eat first thing in the morning and if I'd had to have something so early, it would have been a blueberry muffin and a cappuccino. I had to make do with the oats washed down with the rest of my brew – now stone cold. Still, a cold brew was better than no brew.

'What are we doing today?' Bastion asked.

'Kelpies,' I responded briefly.

'Kelpies,' he repeated dubiously. 'You know about the kelpies?' He sounded surprised.

To the majority of the Other, kelpies are nothing more than a folklore tale. I know the truth, mainly because their image is depicted in Grimmy together with a host of warnings. They are real, and they are lethal.

'Obviously,' I responded drily. Kelpies are a Scottish phenomenon that haunts rivers and streams, usually in the shape of a horse. Their name comes from Gaelic *colpach* or *cailpeach*, meaning colt or heifer, but they are no splashy mares – they are deadly. That is why they have become part of folklore; most people who encounter them don't survive to tell the tale. One of my ancestors had escaped with his skin only because he had a lovely singing voice. Apparently his mournful song had kept the kelpies calm enough for him to back away then run for his life. They had pursued him onto dry land, but eventually the river had called them back and he had escaped with life, limb and some new nightmares. It had been a coincidence that he was singing when he'd seen them, but he believed it had saved him. He'd stopped singing as he slunk away and that's when the pursuit had happened. So in theory all I had to do was sing. Maybe.

'I know where there are some kelpies,' I confirmed. 'Emory took Jinx to see them on their first date.'

Bastion shook his head. 'That man needs to learn more about dating. Kelpies are not first-date territory – or any date territory.' Bastion is rather protective of Jinx; he thinks of her as an honorary niece.

'Really? You're more of a cinema and restaurant man, are you?' My tone was derisive.

'You'd rather kelpies?' he asked incredulously.

'I'd rather originality, thought, effort. It was perfect for Jinx because she's an adrenaline junky.'

'And what would be perfect for you?'

Jake and I hadn't really dated. We were too young when we got together and it was all about house parties and drinking with friends. After the attack he'd been confined to the rental house, hidden away to stay safe from his hunters. No dates then, either.

It was depressing to realise that not only had I never been on a date, I had no idea what my perfect date would be. Harvesting potion ingredients under moonlight with a picnic and fine wine, perhaps? After the harvesting was done, of course; it wouldn't do to drink alcohol and then try and recover the ingredients. That would be a sure-fire way to muck things up.

I shrugged. Maybe dates and I just didn't mix. I was in my forties now, and the time for romance had probably passed me by.

'Are you ready?' Bastion asked. 'The helicopter has arrived.'

I didn't ask how he knew. A lot of the Other creatures have excellent hearing but it feels rude to question them about it. The divide between the humans and the creatures is a touchy issue, and I didn't want to emphasise our differences just before we set out on a dangerous mission. Not that I thought Bastion wouldn't save me, even if I annoyed him; he clearly had his own set of morals, even if they differed from mine.

We went up to the roof. My tote bag was frighteningly empty and I hated not having a plethora of potions at hand, but I needed space for the new ingredients that I would hopefully collect. I had one healing potion and a few brushes, but that was it. I also had several empty water flasks and some Kilner jars; I really hoped we'd be successful.

Inside the helicopter I nodded at Chris in greeting and put on my seatbelt and headset. 'Good morning, Miss DeLea,' he said.

'Morning, Chris.'

'We're heading to Falkirk?'

'Yes, please. To the kelpies.'

'The statues?'

'No, the real ones.'

There was a sigh over the comms. 'I'll be ready for a quick exit then.'

'Probably wise,' I agreed. He started the engine and lifted us upwards.

'What are we going to do with the kelpies?' Bastion asked.

'We're going to collect some water from them. Well, *you* are.'

'You want me to *what*?' He sounded genuinely startled.

'Just swoop on down and collect some of the kelpies' water,' I said patiently. 'The water has to be taken while it is part of a kelpie's form, not before or after.'

'You do realise that kelpies are deadly?'

'Yes, but they're one of the few creatures whose essence we can capture without harming them. They move through water, and as they move they use that water as part of their essence. The sea or the rivers sustain them. We just need some water they are actively using. Taking it won't harm them in the slightest and I'll get the essence of the creature without any of the harm that bloodletting would cause. If we tried to collect blood from a unicorn or a griffin...'

Bastion pressed his lips together. 'We're going to die.'

'Ye of little faith,' I mocked him. 'We'll be fine.' I didn't bother telling him about the singing thing; after all, it was completely untested and only time would tell whether my ancestor's theory was correct. If it was wrong, then we probably *were* going to die.

It might indeed be over when the not-so-fat lady sang.

Chapter 21

There was a tarmac path in front of us. We left Chris and the helicopter at the start of it and started walking. It dwindled into little more than a sheep trail. Luckily I was wearing trainers, the better to run the heck away.

As we trudged, the sheep trail dwindled to undergrowth and mud. That was consistent with Jinx's directions but I felt dubious. How could we be sure we were heading in the right direction? However, I relaxed when I saw two boulders rearing up ahead of us. We were going the right way, assuming that these boulders were the same ones that Jinx had told me about.

I pointed to them and put my forefinger to my lips. Bastion shimmered and suddenly he was in griffin form. His huge lion's body stood higher than my waist and, when his feathered head craned around, he met my eyes with his piercing, golden-eyed stare.

I swallowed hard. Something about griffins always sent a skitter of fear down my spine. I don't know whether it was the deadly claws or the killer beak, but I was hyper-aware that Bastion could destroy me in seconds. I wouldn't have a chance to reach the potion bomb in my pocket. Luckily he didn't seem to want to destroy me, but with a griffin, the urge could come at any time.

We moved forward carefully. Bastion's paws were silent, but my heart was hammering so loudly it must have been audible to creatures far and wide. We climbed up the boulders and, sure enough, there were the kelpies.

Two horse-like figures were frolicking in the river below us. I pulled a plastic bottle from my bag and unscrewed the top. As I held it out to Bastion, I was momentarily stumped because he had no hands to hold it with. My befuddled expression must have given away my thoughts because his sharp eyes seemed to mock me. He reached for the bottle with his front right paw and secured it in his fearsome talons. Then he leaned forward over the water and braced himself to leap down.

I cleared my throat, leaned forward too, and started to sing. I hadn't been sure which song to choose but 'Hallelujah' by Leonard Cohen burst out of me. It was beautiful, and soothing; if that didn't calm the kelpies' violent urges, nothing would.

Bastion's head snapped to mine as my clear alto voice broke the silence. The eyes of both kelpies were fixed on me as I sang, and Bastion stayed in place similarly entranced. I kicked him in the leg as I continued to sing, and he seemed to recollect why we were there. Clutching the bottle, he dived off the boulder towards the creatures waiting below.

Even as he moved ever closer, they were fixed on me – until Bastion dragged the bottle through the mane of one of the kelpies and broke the spell. She threw back her head and whinnied, a sound unlike anything I'd heard before, discordant and threatening. My song faltered and died in my throat. The other kelpie screamed.

'Run!' Bastion yelled. 'I'll lead them away!' His mighty wings were flapping, lifting him higher. I scrambled down the boulder and started to run back the way that we'd come. For a moment I thought that Bastion's plan had worked, but then I heard hooves beating the ground as they got closer and closer to me. I dared not pause or look back. I threw myself forward, cursing my desk-riding, sedentary lifestyle.

I stumbled on the uneven path, stepped into a rut hidden by some overgrown bracken and fell. Heart racing, I scrambled quickly to my feet but I then made the mistake of looking back. I froze at the sight of the watery apparition bearing down on me, nostrils flared in rage.

I stood stock still – incapable of movement as the mare drew closer. I willed myself to move but nothing happened. I'd seen enough of my fair share of magic to know that this was some sort of enchantment and I was caught in its deadly web.

The distance between the kelpie and me was shrinking. As I watched it advance, I felt regret. I wished many things – not that I'd had the chance to finish the potion, but that I had seen Mum again, that I'd told Oscar how much I loved him and how grateful I was for his presence. I should have visited Mum this morning before starting on this venture. I should have told Oscar what he meant to me, though I suspected that he knew. I should have grabbed that drink with Lucy. I should have made a Will to provide for Mum's care. There was a Bastion-thought that I refused to acknowledge. My thoughts were dizzying and my regrets were numerous as death pounded ever nearer to me.

Then claws seized me, wrapping around my waist and yanking me into the air. I gasped as one of them pierced my skin but I had no time to worry about it. I was wrenched upwards as Bastion lifted us high above the kelpie's rearing hooves. She screamed as I was ripped from her grasp and the magic that was freezing me in place melted away, leaving me shuddering at how close death had come.

Bastion flew us to the helicopter before carefully depositing me on the ground. He was still carrying the water bottle in his forepaw, though some of its contents had sloshed out during our panicked flight. Luckily, a good amount remained. I reached into the tote to find the bottle cap and screwed it on.

Bastion shifted onto two legs. 'Are you okay?' he asked urgently.

I nodded. 'Thanks for getting the water.' And saving my life.

'I thought that they would chase me. I'm sorry.'

'Don't be silly,' I said brusquely. 'It's not your fault. Clearly I'm like a polo mint to the kelpies.'

'What?'

'Horses like polo mints,' I explained.

'You always have to explain the best jokes,' he responded drily, but his eyes were still sweeping over me, checking I was okay.

I was glad I was wearing black because the puncture wound in my side was bleeding and I didn't want Bastion to see that he'd hurt me. A quick rune later and I'd be fine. He'd saved my life and he'd feel bad if he realised I was injured; strangely, I didn't want that. Obviously I was afraid that him feeling guilty might impact on him saving me next time. That was all.

'Not the most sustainable potion ingredient,' he remarked.

I shrugged. 'Well, next time we'll ask Lucy to come with us. She can pipe the kelpies.' Lucy is an alpha werewolf and also a piper who can speak to all manner of animals. I'd once seen her pipe an ouroboros so I knew she could communicate with magical creatures, too.

'That's your plan? You're going to get Lucy to ask the kelpies nicely?' he asked incredulously.

'It doesn't cost the kelpies anything to give us some water. I don't see why they'd object.'

'Besides the fact that they're murderous creatures?'

'People in glass houses shouldn't throw stones.' I regretted the sassy retort as soon as it left my mouth. I'd only seen Bastion kill one thing since he'd started protecting me and that was a vampyr that was about to murder me, so it was hard to feel regretful about his death. Besides, the vampyr might have been a puppet for a necromantic black witch and have been grateful to be released.

Bastion didn't respond and my regret deepened. He'd just saved my life and that was how I repaid him? He shimmered into his human form and held out a hand to help me into the helicopter. I took it. As he heaved me in,

I couldn't stop a little gasp as a shard of pain stabbed into me.

'You're hurt,' he said, voice dark. 'I knew I could smell blood. Where?'

I scowled but resistance was futile. At least being open would give me a moment to paint on a healing rune. 'Let's get out of here first,' I suggested.

'Chris, take us up,' Bastion instructed, his eyes not leaving mine. 'Now, show me, witch,' he growled.

I pulled up my black top, revealing the wound.

'My claw,' he muttered. His nostrils flared in self-reproach and his eyes turned golden yellow.

'Before you get lost in self-flagellation, let's not forget that you saved my life. This cut is no big deal.'

'I hurt you!' The words burst out of him.

'It's okay,' I reassured him, a tad confused at the strength of his reaction.

'No, it's not,' he muttered, jaw clenched.

'Well, I'm going to heal myself while you get all worked up.' I opened my tote bag, pulled out the healing potion and quickly painted on *hagalaz* for injury and *sowilo* for health. I pulled a little magic into the runes and then sagged as the pain vanished. Thank the Goddess for magic.

'Where to?' Chris asked.

Ah, yes: a destination would be handy. 'Edinburgh,' I replied.

'You got it.'

Chapter 22

The Court Curiosities shop holds all manner of bric-a-brac. There were some other shoppers, none of whom showed the sign of the Other realm on their foreheads; they were either creatures in human form, or they were straight-up human.

The Verdict, a mysterious magic which rules over *all* of us, compels us to be discreet about the magic realm, so Bastion and I took our time browsing until the shop was emptier. I found a wall of books to get lost in, some old, some new, all pre-loved. I picked up an interesting looking romance and perused the blurb. It was all about a dragon-shifter and a dragon hunter; I love a good enemies-to-lovers romance. It was amusingly entitled *The Dragon's Whored*, which I thoroughly appreciated. I put it down reluctantly as the shop quietened down. Time to get to business.

Tobias, the dragon-shifter behind the till, had already acknowledged me with a solemn nod. He has light-brown hair and blue eyes; he looks a little younger than me but, despite his excellent complexion, his age far exceeds mine. He had supplied my mum with rare potion ingredients since she was an acolyte, so he was at least eighty or ninety years old, but that is nothing in dragon terms. He is still young and impetuous. Despite that, I like him.

When the last human shopper had vacated the tiny premises, I moved forward. 'Amber DeLea,' he greeted me warmly. 'And how go things for the next witch Symposium member?'

'That has yet to be determined,' I said primly.

He waved away my words. 'A foregone conclusion, surely. You're well-liked by the magical community at large.'

'Not as well liked as Kassandra Scholes.'

'She is lovely,' he agreed, 'but she doesn't yet have your... gravitas. You're already a pillar of witch society.'

I liked to think that was true, but I could also see when someone was buttering me up. I sighed. 'What do you need?'

He grinned. 'Perhaps a mutual exchange would be in order? What brings you to my door today?'

HEX OF THE WITCH

I lowered my voice. 'I need you to find me lavender golden wind vervain. And it needs to be a sustainable source.'

He leaned back. 'You're not asking for much,' he said drily. 'Ethically sourced, too?'

'Always.'

He grimaced. 'I can do it. Leave it with me. There are a couple of reclusive growers I can reach out to.'

Some of the older dragons like to hoard plants – potions ingredients, to be precise. Getting it from them as a non-dragon was a non-starter, but Tobias acted as a respectable intermediary when needed. For obvious reasons, getting a dragon to part with his hoard is hard work. The other issue is that the older a dragon gets, the more it loses its grip on reality. Some of the Elder dragons are a tiptoe away from madness – and when they go mad, they become deadly. It is the duty of the Prime dragon to put them down when that happens, but usually it only occurs once in a Prime's reign.

No one knows quite what it is that tips the dragons into insanity, but there are warning signs. The dragons are served by their human families, their brethren, and when they see the signs they are supposed to call in the Prime. I say 'supposed to' because no one wants to be responsible for their great-great-great-great-great-great-great-great-great grandfather's death.

Luckily Tobias is young in the scheme of things, so I would have a good supply of potion ingredients as long as the elusive, reclusive grower didn't kick the bucket anytime soon.

'How much?' I asked Tobias.

'A favour,' he smiled, like it was going to be something simple.

'What and when?'

'Now.'

'What is it?'

He dropped his voice. 'I have an acquaintance who needs some help but he can't afford to pay for it. He won't let me pay either, so you helping him will be a non-starter. He's a proud son of a bitch. I've heard there's a witch called Ellie who has set up a free clinic, and I need him to have a spot there. I know she operates on the down-low but I haven't managed to find out the location yet.' That was because every client of the clinic signed a rune-enforced non-disclosure contract after their appointment.

'What's his name?'

'Brambleford.'

'Imp?'

'Yes.'

I wrote down the address of the clinic and a time slot for my next clinic. 'Tell him to be there at that time. I'll make sure Ellie knows to expect him.'

Tobias took the paper and beamed at me. 'Thank you, Amber! I promise I'll tell him right away so we can get him there in time.' Edinburgh to Slough is quite the journey and imps don't like travelling by human methods; they despise cars and trains – though they enjoy sabotaging them. It is a long distance to travel by foot; perhaps Tobias would offer him a lift in his claws. Dragons don't let anyone but their mates ride on their backs.

'Good. Call me when you have the lavender golden wind vervain.'

'You got it.'

I'd hoped to walk away from his shop with the ingredient but that had probably been too much to ask for.

I gave Tobias one of my rare smiles and left his shop before I could get lost in the shelves, browsing the old books that graced the walls and smelled of adventures, hope and love. Bastion loitered a moment longer, talking quietly with Tobias.

I had just stepped out of the Court Curiosities when my phone rang. The phone number was withheld. I swiped to answer.

'Princess, did you honestly come all the way to Edinburgh and *not* call me?'

I felt myself smile. 'Aunt Abigay,' I said, exasperated. 'I literally just arrived.'

'Humph. That's not how I hear it.' Her tone grew solemn. 'You are instructed to appear before the council. I can't be there, so don't be late.' She hung up without giving me a time.

Bastion stepped out of the shop as I disconnected the call. 'Oh fudge,' I muttered.

Bastion raised one eyebrow. 'Problem?'

'The council wants to see me.'

'When?'

'I didn't get a time, so that means now.'

'Let's go then.'

I hated being summoned like I was little more than an acolyte, but when the council click their fingers you jump *before* you ask 'how high?'.

I had spent a fair amount of time in Edinburgh during my training, so I knew the way. I led Bastion towards Edinburgh Castle and stopped when we reached The Witchery. The council takes hiding in plain sight to a whole new level.

The Witchery is a fine-dining restaurant and, like most things the witches are involved in, it is incredibly expensive. The food is second to none though, and the income it generates helps covens in need; the witches look after their own.

It was too early for customers when I pushed open the heavy wooden door. The staff were buzzing around preparing for lunch service, and seeing the acolytes rushing around made me smile to myself. I remembered my time at the Witchery with fondness; the tips had been impressive, and it was one of the few times in my life that I'd enjoyed the camaraderie that came from working together for an extended period of time. No familiars were allowed on the Witchery floor so my lack of one hadn't been so noticeable.

The interior design tended towards dark-wood panelling, red-leather seats and lots of tall candles ensconced in gold candlesticks. Fresh white linen was being laid on the tables and the silverware was being carefully placed. The maître d', a stern witch called Rosemary, greeted me. 'Amber. You're expected. Go on down.' She looked at Bastion. 'Alone,' she added pointedly.

'Stay here,' I directed Bastion.

He frowned unhappily. 'You are no safer here than anywhere else.'

'If the council wanted me dead, they wouldn't have hired you,' I pointed out logically. 'Stay, have a drink. Entertain the acolytes.'

'I will watch the door for threats,' he said, his jaw set to stubborn.

'You must be fun at parties.'

'I am not.'

I found myself smiling as I descended the stairs into the basement.

Chapter 23

An elaborate underground city exists beneath Edinburgh. For centuries it remained hidden and buried, the way the witches preferred it. Then, in the 1990s, a bunch of Common realm entrepreneurial digs were carried out that exposed old vaults, houses and more. Nowadays a small portion of the seventeenth-century streets is exposed to tourists via colourful tours that cite horrifying history. The excavated streets lie beneath the Royal Mile. Luckily, the witches were able to rune off some sections and hide them from the Common realmers, leaving us free to stalk the subterranean passages largely unchecked.

I stole down the basement stairs and into the hidden city. Electricity had been one of the last modern conveniences to make its way here, and I was grateful that the passageways had modern lighting. It was far less creepy when the underground streets were lit up.

I pushed myself back against the wall as another witch made her way past me. 'Coven Mother,' she murmured, giving me a little curtsey. I inclined my head in recognition of the respect, but the woman wasn't someone I knew.

I fingered the potion bomb in my pocket. Using it down here would have disastrous – and deadly – consequences. At times, the underground city felt like it was one good sneeze away from being destroyed and being buried alive was not on the list of ways I wanted to die.

I came to one of the larger spaces, a square between the passages. Tables were laden with potions or their ingredients. You could find most things for the right price at the underground market. I wanted to browse, but the coven council wouldn't be thrilled if I delayed presenting myself. As I walked on, I vowed to stop on my way back. I needed a sustainable source of lavender vervain, not just a one-off pouch – though a one-off pouch might at least get me started while Tobias negotiated with his growers. Tobias was the smart choice but the slower one, and Goddess knows I'm an impatient soul.

As I hustled through the corridors, I was stopped numerous times to be greeted or questioned on the best potion for this or that ailment. I resisted the urge to direct them to the coven library and answered their questions patiently. It was nice to be respected and I'd worked hard to earn it, despite my handicap of not having a familiar.

At last I reached the council chambers. The door was guarded by a golem called Benjamin Cohen. He stood a solid six-feet five-inches tall, his roughhewn body made of clay and runes. He was dressed in a black T-shirt and black suit trousers, and his huge feet were enclosed in specialist boots. Benjamin was kept largely underground for the witches' eyes only. I had long suspected that he must feel as lonely and isolated as I often did.

'Benjamin,' I greeted him.

'Amber DeLea.' His deep, rumbling voice poured out of his heavy chest and his thick lips twitched in what passed for a smile. 'Are you well?'

'I am, thank you.' I reached out to touch his arm. His skin felt cold and clammy, like wet rock after a thunderstorm. I had observed that others didn't often touch him – whether out of fear or revulsion, I didn't know – but he leaned into the barest touch. I always made the effort to give him some of the human contact that he so clearly craved.

'How are you, Benjamin?' I asked. I'd petitioned the council more than once to let my coven take care of him, but he was too useful here in this dark, dank place surrounded by the ground he was made of.

'I am experimenting with being called Benji,' he said finally.

'Would you like me to call you that?' I asked gently.

He nodded. 'Yes. You are a friend. A friend should have a nickname. I am Benji, friend.'

My heart ached a little; he had no nickname for me. 'You can call me Am, Benji,' I found myself saying.

His lips curved up and there was no denying his smile now. 'Am,' he rumbled with satisfaction. Then his smile faded. 'You must be careful here, Am. Not everyone is your friend.'

I patted him again on the arm. 'I know.'

'I have noticed that friends often give each other nicknames that rhyme. I could call you Am-Bam. It is clever because it rhymes and it is close to your actual name, which is Am-Ber.'

My mouth dropped open, but as I looked up at his hopeful eyes I found I couldn't refuse him. Goddess help me if he ever said it in front of other people – it made me sound like a Flintstone. Yabba-dabba-doo! 'Maybe keep that one private, just for us,' I suggested lightly.

'Like a *secret* name?'

'Exactly.'

Looking impressed, Benji nodded. He moved aside to let me go inside the chamber. As I stepped past him, his huge tree-trunk arms reached out and drew me into a hug. His body was hard and cold, but I hugged him back as hard as I could, chill be damned.

'Friends hug, Am-Bam,' he murmured into my hair and I felt the vibrations of his words through his mighty chest. The witches who had made him had done an astonishing job, and I felt somewhat smug since I was one of them. I had worked incredibly hard on the golem and Benji was proof that I was indeed a genius.

Benji's quiet use of my new nickname made my heart ache even more. I wondered if he had invited anyone else to call him Benji, or if it was us two rejects against the world. 'They do hug,' I agreed, as if I had loads of friends and knew what they did.

I felt tension slide from my shoulders. How long had it been since I had last hugged someone? I couldn't say.

Benji released me and patted my back, which nearly sent me sprawling. Luckily his hand shot out and caught me before I hit the floor. 'Sorry,' he said, embarrassed. 'I'm clumsy.'

I did my best to smile reassuringly. 'It's fine, Benji, really. I'd best go in.'

He nodded and pulled the door open for me. I walked through and tried not to wince as it closed ominously behind me. I couldn't help but wish I had Bastion with me.

Chapter 24

The coven's council chamber was deliberately dimly lit but, unlike the other rooms, it was at least furnished. A host of ornately carved wooden chairs were set out in a semi-circle in front of a raised dais. Facing them, a plain, unvarnished chair sat in the centre of the room on a blood-red rug. No doubt the rug had a pentagram beneath it with compulsive truth runes activated – I'd learned my chair trick from the best. As soon as I walked forward, I felt the urge to spill my secrets.

The whole room stank of power play and politics, and I couldn't wait to be on the other side of this BS.

I gritted my teeth and sat down. There were thirteen chairs in front of me. The middle one, which was larger and grander than the rest, was empty. It was that chair which I coveted most; it symbolised not just a place on the council but on the Symposium itself – the ruling body of the Connection.

Some of the occupants were missing from the semi-circle but seven witches were present, the minimum number for the council to be convened. Each witch had a cowl drawn up to keep their face in shadow. My alter ego 'Ellie Tron' had got the idea for a seer-spelled cloak from here, too.

The cowls were meant both to intimidate and to provide anonymity, though few witches were concerned about that. Virtually every member was open about their position on the council these days now that there was much less fear of witch-hunts.

The lights in the chamber had been angled so that they shone into my eyes. Each council chair, save mine, had its own lectern that acted as a physical barrier. I had nothing; my body was exposed to their runes and their eyes. Whoever had designed this chamber understood psychology and had used it to devastating effect. I resisted the urge to shuffle in my seat.

I know a fair amount about psychology too. They had summoned *me,* so let them speak first. I assumed a polite smile, folded my hands on my lap and waited. The moment stretched, getting more painful. The truth compulsion was tickling my spine and the urge to spill something – anything – was rising. I shoved it down stubbornly and kept my hands still.

Eventually someone cleared their throat. 'As delightful as this is,' an American voice drawled, 'I'm sure we all have places to be.'

I recognised the voice right away: Willow Blackwood. I had worked hard to win her favour; when her familiar had fallen ill, I'd managed not only to bring the cat back to good health but to optimum condition. She wasn't a friend per se, but I hoped she was an ally.

'Miss DeLea,' Willow continued, 'the council wishes for an update on your progress. Please explain what forward steps you have made since your application was approved.'

I blinked. I'd had one day since Kassandra Scholes had arrived to take over my mantle so surely they didn't expect my potion to be ready. Absurd. I cleared my throat. 'I have managed to acquire some essential ingredients that I hope will allow me to finalise the potion.'

'What is your estimated brew time?' a hard voice snapped out. Arthur Starling, I thought.

'I am still sourcing further ingredients. After the final ones are collected, I estimate the potion will be ready soon.' There, that was nice and vague; if I didn't promise a date then I couldn't fail to deliver on it.

'What ingredients are you sourcing?' Tristan asked. His tone was offhand but he was leaning forward eagerly in his seat so his body language was at odds with his voice. The truth runes leaned on me and I struggled against them; the ingredients weren't for public knowledge, not before my patent was in place.

Willow scoffed, 'Nice try, Tristan. She's not going to tell you the ingredients. Her potion is her information until it is complete, tested – and available for a price.' She turned to me. 'How are you, Amber?' She was giving me another question that the truth rune could latch onto, one that I could actually answer. I could have hugged her as the compulsion to spill the truth about the ingredients fell away and turned to something that I could answer easily.

'I'm fine, thank you,' I answered truthfully then stifled a gasp as the weight of the truth rune left me.

'How are things going with the griffin?' Seren Songbird asked. I'd recognise her lilting voice anywhere.

'Not too badly,' I said evenly. The truth rune leaned on me again. 'He's okay,' I admitted. *What?* What the hell was that? He was *okay?* I hated him, right? He was Satan incarnate, although I wasn't sure that Satan would sleep under my bed to make me feel better. I tried to keep the inner turmoil off my face.

Seren slumped back in her chair, 'Well, what a relief,' she muttered. I had no doubt that if she were sitting on my chair, she couldn't have said that while under the force of the truth runes. She had disliked me since we were acolytes together.

When I thought of bullies, I pictured Seren; tall, willowy and perfect, she had made my life hell as soon as she'd found out I didn't have a familiar. Freak was probably the nicest thing she'd called me. She was immature and rumour suggested she'd slept her way to her council seat, supposedly by wooing Tristan. When she had her seat, she'd dropped him faster than you can say 'gold digger', though the 'gold' in question was a place on the council. She was one of the few people in my life that deserved the moniker that rhymed with 'witch'.

'We're not here to talk about potions and griffins,' Carl snarled impatiently. Even with the cowl casting shadows on his face, I fancied that I could still see the white beard covering his weak chin. I recognised the bite in his bark. He continued, 'We're here to talk about the rumour that you have a black witch in your midst.'

Oh damn. 'Allegedly,' I said faintly.

'It's not that "alleged" when they walk in and place a bloody bomb under your bed. If you hadn't spent the night at the portal, we'd still be scraping your brains off your ceiling!'

That was a visual I could do without. Denial was my friend – if I thought too long about my near-death experience I'd freak out – but it was hard to do denial when Carl was determined to paint a bloody van Gogh in my mind.

'Investigations are under way,' I said firmly. 'If a black witch is operating in my coven I'll find them.' Technically investigations were under way, but the truth was I hadn't focused much on them because the potion and the attacks on my life had distracted me. Well, no more: I had my sights set on this black witch. The potion would have to take a back seat for a while. I couldn't do both.

'We are going to appoint the investigation to Kassandra Scholes since you're so busy with your potion,' Seren said snidely.

I scowled. 'I can do both,' I said as evenly as I could, despite the fact that I'd just admitted to myself that I couldn't. I was surprised that the truth runes had let me utter that statement; obviously deep down I *did* believe I could do both.

'Can you?' Carl countered. 'You're the one who requested a temporary Coven Mother to step into the breach. Your potion has to be the priority – we can't afford to have your focus elsewhere. If you really can significantly increase our time in the Other, that is far more important than one black witch.'

'One black witch can wreak havoc,' I countered. 'There is already evidence that he or she has controlled some vampyrs.'

'Necromancy,' Willow spat. 'We can't have this getting out. The Red Guard will be all over it.' The Red Guard is the vampyr equivalent of the SS; they're violent and they think the ends justify the means. I'd rubbed shoulders with them a couple of times and each experience had been uncomfortable.

All necromancers start as witches. They use death to fuel their runes, and in the sliding scale of evil they stand at the top. It is a slippery slope from being a blood-magic user to becoming a black witch and using pain in spell work – and then using death.

Since necromancers can control the dead – including vampyrs – the Red Guard eye all witches with suspicion. I'd been threatened by them a time or two and they had told me they had their eye on me. Well, they could watch all they wanted because I would *never* use someone's pain or death to fuel a spell. It was just plain wrong.

'I'm the more experienced investigator and I know my coven. If one of them is slipping, I'll find them faster than Kassandra.' I resisted labouring the point further. I needed to be the one who dealt with this; these were my people and they were my responsibility. The potion, and the fame and glory that would come with it, would have to wait. It was time to go on a witch-hunt.

Chapter 25

I asked the council politely if I could take Benji back to my coven with me. As usual they refused, but they did at least agree that I could have three days to find the black witch. After that, they would give the case to Kassandra.

Kassandra Scholes is annoyingly competent and I had no doubt that she'd locate the witch if that were her sole task, but I wanted her focused on running the coven, training the acolytes and balancing our books and resources. Besides, I didn't need yet another mark in her plus column in the competition to become the witch Symposium member.

Benji looked up hopefully as I walked out of the chamber then tried not to look downcast when I shook my head. I tapped his cold hand. 'Sorry,' I murmured. 'I did ask.'

'It's fine,' he rumbled. It wasn't, but there wasn't anything I could do about it at that moment. One day I would hopefully have more say in Benji's future. There were so many people I could help if only I had a little more power. Once I was safely ensconced in the Symposium, I intended to change the rules so that I could officially start a free clinic for healing. I believe that healthcare should be available to everyone, not dependent on the size of your wallet. Everyone deserves an equal chance at having a long, healthy, life.

'I'll walk you out,' Benji offered. 'Carl said you're in danger.'

I suppressed a grimace at the dramatic phrasing, though he wasn't wrong. 'I always welcome your company, Benji,' I said. 'I just want to pop to the underground market on the way back.'

I was grateful for Benji's lumbering presence because it felt odd not to have Bastion with me. In just a couple of days I'd grown used to someone dogging my steps. He led the way and I ambled behind his wide frame; in some places he almost filled the narrow corridors that lay beneath the city.

We were approaching the market when a sharp intake of breath behind me made my neck prickle. I turned around just as an ogre slammed a metal mace down towards my face.

I tapped the watch on my wrist, pulled my power into it and accessed the Third realm. The Third realm controls time, and the witches had runed some objects to link with its portal. The objects were heavily regulated and given mostly to the Connection's inspectors. My watch was a highly illegal gift from Mum, who had long been fascinated by the Third realm.

I tugged on the link to the Third realm to slow time and, as that happened, I pulled the potion bomb from my pocket. I hesitated before I activated it – if I lit it here, we'd collapse the damned tunnel. Who knew how many people would be trapped or injured?

The mace moved slowly, gradually getting closer to my face. I shouldn't have hesitated because the small burst of the Third realm was already dissipating and the link was fading. I started to turn so that the mace would strike my shoulder rather than my face. The blow would still hurt like a bitch but hopefully I'd survive it – and it was better that I got hurt than others died because I'd activated the potion. Then everything sped up into real time and the mace was swinging down at me. I braced myself.

But even as I turned, Benji was moving faster than seemed possible for a hunk of rock. Suddenly he was beside me and, with an inarticulate rumble of rage, his stone-like arm hovered in front of me to protect me from the blow. Sparks flew as the metal mace crashed against him.

There was nowhere to go. I was stuck between a golem and an ogre – literally stuck between a rock and hard place. The only weapon I had was a potion bomb that would kill all three of us in the narrow corridor. I had nothing in my arsenal but panic. I should at least have been carrying my athame; it was a foolish omission and one I heartily regretted.

All ogres have grotesque twisted features and bodies. The one facing us had a huge right shoulder and an extra-large left eye that bulged out of his skull, making him look very surprised. Maybe he *was* surprised; he'd probably expected to encounter my unguarded back rather than a rageful golem. And Benji *was* full of rage. His eyes burned with fury and, as he shifted from being defensive to offensive, his fingers fused together and lengthened to form a single, deadly spike.

The ogre was eight-feet tall and that should have given him a long reach, but he was hunched over in the confined space of the tunnel and had no room to pull back his mace to deliver another blow. He threw it aside and reached for a blade instead, but Benji was quicker. He reached around me and struck the ogre's overly large eye with his newly sharpened limb.

The ogre gave a cry as the stone sword penetrated his eye and his skull, then he fell silent as he staggered back and fell to the floor.

My heart was hammering and the instinct to flee was almost overwhelming, but I needed to calm the heck down and stay the course. I took several deep breaths and my stomach roiled as I breathed in the coppery blood smell of the dead man before me. Dead because of me.

'Is he definitely dead?' I asked Benji. Maybe the sword hadn't penetrated too deeply? Perhaps I could heal him and question him? I didn't want to step closer to my would-be murderer to check.

Benji reached out and sliced the ogre's throat. 'Definitely,' he confirmed with satisfaction as sluggish blood trickled onto the ground.

I blinked. 'I was thinking about questioning him,' I explained.

'Ah. Well ... no. You won't be able to do that.' We both looked at the thoroughly deceased corpse.

'No,' I agreed drily. 'It looks like I won't.'

'I saved you though!' Benji sounded excited.

'You did.' A smile curved my lips despite the dire situation. 'Thank you so much, Benji.'

'You're welcome Am-Bam.' He grinned at me triumphantly.

I was grateful that the only witness to that nickname was cooling on the floor. I always try to find the silver linings; staring at the bloody corpse, that was the only one I could think of.

Someone had tried to kill me and only luck had kept me alive. Bastion was going to be pissed off, and I wasn't too thrilled either. I wasn't safe even in Edinburgh, the witches' stronghold. Enemies were popping up everywhere and I was notoriously rubbish at whack-a-mole.

I needed to get better or I was going to get killed.

Chapter 26

Bastion vibrated with barely contained fury. 'What?' he growled, his voice low and deadly.

'I was attacked by an ogre,' I repeated. 'With a mace. Benji saved me, though, so it was fine.'

'It was fine?' he echoed incredulously.

Maybe fine was the wrong word. 'All's well that ends well,' I said brightly. The phrase made me think of Mum and my heart ached. I needed to see her; there is nothing like a strong dose of fear to get you running to your mum. 'Shall we go?'

After the attack I'd insisted that Benji still take me to the market, where we'd searched for the rare strain of vervain with no luck. I'd been so sure that I'd find *something* there and it was rare for the underground market to let me down. Hopefully Tobias would come through; that dragon could acquire anything for the right price. If the price was too high, I'd get the council to cough up the rest. The meagre grant they had offered at the start of the project had barely accounted for one quarter of my ingredients, but I didn't want to rock the boat too much by asking for more, not when I was hoping for the Symposium position. Soon they would announce the shortlist and I had no doubt I'd be on it, then it was a small matter of a few exams and Am-Bam – congratulations, ma'am.

Dream big or go home.

Bastion was staring at me, his jaw working as he fought to keep his temper under control. 'I'm not leaving you now, not even for the damned council.'

I didn't know quite what to say, so I said nothing. Bastion followed me as we entered the restaurant again. I ignored the way several of the acolytes batted their eyelashes at him and started twirling their hair around their fingers. I was gratified to note that he was ignoring them just as studiously as I was.

'Is she in?' I asked the maître d' and nodded towards the stairs.

She nodded. 'She's expecting you.'

Of course she was. I headed upstairs. The rooms above the restaurant were available for hire; at nearly a thousand pounds per night they weren't cheap, but they were luxurious. No wonder the Crone had ensconced herself there – plus she loved the food that she could sneak down and steal from the kitchen. There are perks to being old and having very few effs to give.

I knocked on her door. 'Come in, Amber,' she called. I entered with Bastion following on my heels.

'Do we need witnesses for this conversation?' she asked mildly, gesturing at him. Her lips shone with a bright-pink lipstick and her eyes were twinkling with mischief. When I grow up, I want to be exactly like Aunt Abigay.

Before I could reply, Bastion growled, 'She was attacked in the underground city after your council made me stay behind.'

'You think someone in the council is behind the attacks?' The Crone leaned forward intently.

'Don't you?' Bastion shot back. 'Someone accidentally leaks a document and suddenly the attacks start? No. It's all happening too fast. Hiring assassins takes time. We get the file, we verify the information, we scout ahead, we plan and observe. Only then do we attack.'

'You're assuming a level of professionalism that Amber's assassins may not have. Not every killer is a griffin,' Aunt Abigay pointed out.

'This time the attacker was an ogre. Luckily he brought a mace to fight with in a confined space. If he'd actually been prepared... ' He trailed off and grimaced.

I scowled; if it hadn't been for Benji... 'I should carry my athame,' I muttered.

'You'll be carrying more than that the next time we go out,' Bastion promised darkly.

'She won't need it if she has you,' Aunt Abigay said.

Bastion shook his head. 'We can be separated or overwhelmed by attackers. She needs to be able to protect herself.'

'I have a potion bomb,' I pointed out.

'Which you didn't use,' he said flatly.

'Well ... no. It would have collapsed the tunnel onto our heads.'

'Exactly. You need more than one weapon in your arsenal.'

'I have you.'

His eyes darkened. 'You do.'

Aunt Abigay was grinning. 'Well, you two seem to be getting on better.'

I scowled. 'We're not here to talk about Bastion; we're here to talk about the council. Someone has hired people to kill me and I need suspects. Is there anyone you don't trust on the council?'

As the Crone, Abigay operated outside the council. The Crone is there to advise, but she can't vote in council matters though in reality her guiding words pretty much dictate the outcome of the vote. Her position is respected because she has the Goddess's visions to guide and inform her; only a fool ignores the Crone. The Mother and the Maiden are different. Those positions only have a tenure of a year or two because as the witches age they are no longer the optimal ages for those roles. Not so with the Crone; it is the only lifelong role available to a witch.

Aunt Abigay flashed me a smile. 'Is there anyone I don't trust?' She snorted. 'Better to ask me who I *do* trust!'

'Well? Who do you trust?'

'Willow and Hilary.'

'That's it? That's the whole list?' I demanded incredulously. Hilary Mitchell hadn't been on the council today, but she was an ornery old witch who was a little older than Aunt Abigay. They were friends, two old birds of a feather snarking away together.

'That's it,' Abigay agreed grimly, her humour fading. 'There are others I like, but I only *trust* those two. Who turned up for your council session today?'

'Arthur Starling, Willow Blackwood, Tristan Farhand, Seren Songbird, Carl Greenwood,' I listed.

'That's only five. Who else?'

I shrugged helplessly. 'I don't know. The other two didn't speak.'

'They had their cowls up?' She raised an eyebrow.

'Yes.'

Her frown deepened. 'They don't usually do that for the Coven Mothers these days. I'll see what I can find out. It's telling that *I* wasn't summoned to attend the meeting.' Her lips tightened into a grim line. 'I respected that decision because my relationship with you is well known, but perhaps I shouldn't have. Leave it with me. I'll find out who else was there today.'

'You think whoever ordered the hit was at the meeting?' Bastion asked sharply.

'You don't? Someone knew exactly where Amber would be and managed to smuggle in and hide an ogre until it was time for an attack. Believe me, I'll be looking into how that happened.' Anger crackled in her voice.

'Be careful,' I urged her. 'I don't want you sticking your head in a bees' nest.'

She waved away my caution. 'I've been stung many times in my life – I can handle it.' Her gaze sharpened. 'Now what are you doing about this black witch of yours?'

I sighed. 'Honestly? The whole thing feels a little ... amateurish.'

'Someone cancelled the runes and planted a bomb in your room,' Bastion protested. 'That's not mucking about.'

'No, but the thing with Ada and Frankie... Why didn't they hurt Frankie? If it's a necromancer who can control vampyrs, why leave him alive? Whoever this black witch is – or witches are – they could have harnessed his life energy to become even more powerful but instead they let him sleep.'

'You think there's more than one black witch?' Abigay asked.

I nodded. 'I do. When Bastion's daughter was kidnapped, I found her covered in complex, well-drawn runes. Someone experienced had done them – but some of the recent things I've seen have come from amateur hour.'

The first clue I'd had that there was a black witch in my midst was Fehu fluttering into my life with both wings broken. A true black witch would have kept him caged and fed off his pain for an extended period before killing him. Instead, he'd managed to escape.

'A black witch and an acolyte?' Bastion suggested.

I nodded reluctantly; that was the conclusion I'd reached. 'A pair, at least.'

'What are you going to do about it?' Abigay quirked a thick white eyebrow in challenge.

'I'm going to catch them,' I confirmed grimly.

'How?'

'I'm going to set a trap.' I cracked my knuckles. My adversaries weren't going to know what hit them – because if they did, they'd counter it and then I'd be screwed.

Chapter 27

The helicopter had us back in England within a couple of hours. Bastion and I didn't speak as we contemplated the numerous difficult tasks ahead of us. I stared dully at the scenery beneath us as I tried to fine-tune my plans, even though I knew those plans would be chucked out of the window when the poop hit the fan.

Night was drawing in and I concluded reluctantly that it was too late to disturb Mum. She grew tired early these days, and visiting in the evening was always difficult for her. I wanted to see her but it would be selfish to do so.

Chris landed the helicopter on the coven roof and left with a cheery wave. He was entirely too chirpy for my liking; I didn't trust anyone who was so cheerful. It wasn't natural; drugs had to be involved.

Bastion and I returned to my flat. I sent Oscar a quick message to let him know I was safely back in the coven tower. *Anything to report?* came his instant response.

I hesitated. He would worry if he knew about the ogre, but I try not to lie to him; he has a thing about being lied to, and an omission is just as bad in his eyes.

An incident with an ogre. Nothing serious. I downplayed it as much as I could.

Shall I come up? I can sleep on your sofa.

No need. Bastion hasn't let me out of his sight since then.

But he did in Edinburgh? The accusation came through loud and clear.

He was ordered to by the coven council. I didn't know why I was defending Bastion, but it wasn't his fault. *I had Benjamin with me. I'm fine.*

I'm coming up.

I sighed aloud and Bastion raised an eyebrow in question. 'Oscar's coming up. He's not happy about the ogre thing.'

Surprise crossed his face, there and gone in an instant. 'You told him about that?'

'I try not to lie to Oscar. I respect him.'

'You love him,' he corrected insightfully.

That too, but I didn't need to be mushy about it. There was a brisk knock on the door before Oscar let himself in. He started in on Bastion before he'd even cleared the threshold. 'You let her wander around the underground city *alone*?'

'Not my choice,' Bastion responded stiffly. 'Technically the council is my employer.'

'Well, let's rectify that right now. Quit the council and I'll hire you!' Oscar stated.

I snorted. 'You can't afford his rates.'

'That's between me and Bastion. And what were you thinking, leaving your bodyguard behind after someone had just planted a bomb in your flat?' Anger laced his tone but I knew it was there because he loved me.

I crossed the distance between us and gave him another of my rare hugs; I'd have to be careful or people would start thinking that I was a hugger. 'Sorry I scared you, but I'm okay.'

His shoulders dropped. 'This time,' he whispered. He kissed me on the forehead. 'You're okay *this time*. Am, you've got to take better care of yourself.'

'I will, I promise. I won't let Bastion leave me again.'

'I didn't *leave* you,' Bastion objected. 'You left me.'

'Semantics.' I gave Oscar one last squeeze and excused myself to use the bathroom. When I returned, tension was vibrating between the two men. I looked between them. 'What did I miss?'

'Nothing,' they both said at once, but when Oscar looked at me he seemed strangely disappointed.

I snorted in disbelief. I would have pressed the issue further but a tap at my window distracted me and galvanised Bastion into action. Someone was at my balcony door. The griffin looked out, then expelled a sharp breath. 'It's just the raven.'

'Fehu? Let him in.'

Bastion opened the door. Fehu flew in and circled the room before settling on my shoulder. 'Your familiar?' Oscar breathed.

The hope in his voice and his eyes cut my heart to ribbons. 'No.' I tried to keep my voice level. 'Not mine. He belongs to someone, but not to me.'

'You can't just let someone else's familiar in here!' Oscar huffed. 'What if he's working against you?'

'He's not,' I argued. 'There's no ill-intent in Fehu.'

Oscar threw up his hands in exasperation. 'There may not be any ill will in the damned bird, but what about in his owner? For all we know, it could be the black witch's familiar.'

'No,' I said firmly. 'The first time I met him, the black witch had hurt him – snapped his wings.'

'That could have been a ploy. How did the bird get to you with his wings snapped? He could have been planted,' Oscar set his hands on his hips.

'He's mine,' Bastion interrupted.

'What?' Oscar demanded, startled.

'He's my familiar,' Bastion repeated.

Something in me ached; so even Bastion had a familiar. I started to battle a dismay so strong that it took my breath away. I didn't want Fehu to be Bastion's familiar, I wanted him to be mine.

When I was sure I could speak without sobbing I said, 'But you're not a witch!' Anger replaced my dismay. How the hell did Bastion have a familiar? Life was often unfair, but this was one giant slap in the face with a rotting fish.

'Obviously not.' Bastion shot me a condescending look.

'You should have told me he was your familiar!' I snarled.

'Why? What difference would it have made?'

He had me there. My rage slipped away, leaving me feeling bereft. What difference would it have made? None, except perhaps I would have guarded my heart a little more and kept my hopes low, low, low. 'It's important to know things like that,' I responded lamely. Then I went on the attack; the best defence is a good offensive. 'How? How did he become your familiar?'

Bastion's skin tone warmed and he cleared his throat awkwardly. 'When I was younger and learning how to coax, I practised on animals. One day I got cocky and I went too deep. I created a bond between us.'

I stared at him, then at Fehu. When Bastion was young? 'How old is Fehu?'

'About two hundred years old, give or take. We didn't keep accurate records in those days.'

Fehu gave a kraa and hopped up and down on my shoulder before nuzzling my neck. In a daze, I reached up to stroke his plumage. 'Two hundred,' I said in disbelief. I glared at Bastion. 'All this time I've been calling him Fehu. What's his real name?'

'Raven.'

'You named your raven Raven?'

'I was expecting him to die in a few years. I didn't want to get too attached,' he explained.

'You didn't want to get attached to your familiar? Well, it's safe to say that didn't work out,' I said drily.

Fehu gave a happy trill, flew from my shoulder to Bastion's and nuzzled him. Bastion's dark eyes softened and I saw a trace of humanity in them. 'No, it didn't,' he agreed – and deliberately ruffled Fehu's feathers the wrong way.

The raven gave an outraged squawk and nipped Bastion's ear in protest, then settled down to the laborious task of arranging his feathers just so. It had the feeling of an age-old ritual, and Bastion's eyes were still soft. So even

Bastion had a familiar. I had clearly been a witch with a 'b' instead of a 'w' in a past life.

I left Bastion, Fehu and Oscar to talk and went into my office. My old childhood wounds were being picked at and I needed a moment. I stared at my dull reflection on the blank screen. 'It doesn't matter that you don't have a familiar,' I whispered. I was furious when a tear rolled down my cheek. I brushed it away firmly and turned on my computer. I had no time for self-pity. I needed to woman up.

As always when life feels empty, I threw myself into work. That was somewhere that I could make a difference. I logged into my computer and checked my emails to see how Kassandra had been spending her time. She'd called a coven meeting, which I'd missed, but Meredith had kindly emailed me the minutes. Nothing alarming stood out. Begrudgingly, I had to admire Kassandra's efficiency and her ability to go into a new place and get stuck in. She was no wallflower.

She and her assistant, Becky, had also politely cc'd me into a bunch of emails. I reluctantly had to conclude that she knew what she was doing. Dammit.

A message from Tobias told me he'd made contact with his grower and things looked favourable. He would update me tomorrow. I emailed Janice and set up an appointment for the imp Tobias had told me about. I didn't put Brambleford's name on the email – names aren't used at the clinic because anonymity is so important – but at least she'd know to reserve him a slot. We always allow for a number of walk-ins; not every emergency in life comes neatly scheduled.

I tried to quash my impatience. I wanted to get started on the potion now and add the kelpie water, but it wouldn't do any good without the vervain to balance it. Patience was key but it was in short supply. I needed to get this potion finished before someone finished me.

Chapter 28

The polite knock on the door sent a jolt through me that made me realise I'd been snoozing. I was no longer young enough to burn the candles at both ends. 'What?' I called out, hastily wiping the drool from my face.

'It's late. You should go to bed and get some sleep,' Bastion called through the door.

I bit down the snarky comment that he was my bodyguard, not my nursemaid. Yes, I had been asleep but sleeping hunched over your desk isn't as comfortable as sprawling in a bed. I wanted to refuse because it was his idea – but I really did want to go to bed.

Stubbornly, I worked for five more minutes then locked up my office and prepared for some much-needed shut-eye. Bastion walked into my bedroom wearing jogging trousers and nothing else. His body was covered in a fine sheen of sweat; it was clear that he'd been working out while I'd been just plain working.

'I'll shower but I won't be long,' he said gruffly and disappeared into the bathroom.

I turned to the bed and stopped. On top of my pillow was the book I'd been browsing at Court Curiosities, *The Dragon's Whored*. My mouth dropped open and stayed that way. Bastion had bought me a book I'd wanted, even though once before he'd smirked derisively at my romance novels.

I didn't know what to think of that, so I decided not to think about it at all. Instead, I slid into the sheets and started to read about the huntress who was going to get her dragon in more ways than one. I slid into escapism and my troubles fell away.

I was absorbed in the book, but when Bastion strolled out with a towel hooked around his waist I was momentarily distracted from my page. He sauntered forward to retrieve his holdall from under the bed, snagged a pair of black boxer shorts and disappeared back into the bathroom. It was then that I realised I'd been staring the *whole* time.

My face reddened with embarrassment and I wished with all my might for the bed to swallow me whole. Maybe he hadn't noticed? Yeah, right: the hyper-vigilant assassin didn't notice me staring at his abs. Ugh. I hit myself in the face with my book and felt no better.

I was still groaning to myself when Bastion strolled out again. This time I kept my eyes firmly glued to the page. Just because he looked nice didn't mean I should ogle. No one likes to be judged for their looks alone – except maybe runway models. They probably don't mind it so much. I realised I had been staring at the same page for too long and hastily turned to the next. *Focus, Amber.*

I was jolted out of my thoughts when Bastion grabbed a pillow and rolled under the bed. I opened my mouth to tell him he didn't need to bother but closed it again. I opened my mouth to thank him for the book but nothing came out. I grimaced and tried again. Third time lucky, right? 'Goodnight, Bastion.' My voice was a little high-pitched and breathy, but it was better than nothing.

'Good night, Amber. Don't read too late.'

I had been about to set the book down but instead I kept reading until my eyes were gritty and sore, only giving up when it fell onto my face for the second time. I checked the time: 2am. Ouch. I was going to regret this tomorrow. Today. Still, I'd thoroughly enjoyed the tension between the characters and I'd chuckled at the huntress's complete ignorance of the dragon's very obvious feelings for her. If only life were so simple.

As I shut off my alarm and threw my phone across the room in a fit of pique, I heard a rumbling laugh beneath me. 'Good morning, Amber.'

I stifled a yawn. 'Good morning.'

'How was the book?' His voice was knowing.

'Too good,' I muttered. 'Thank you,' I added begrudgingly.

'You're very welcome.' He rolled out from underneath the bed and went to the bathroom as I continued loafing under the bedcovers. I pulled my journal from the bedside table and quickly scrawled a few lines of gratitude: *I'm grateful my mum is alive. I'm grateful for Oscar. I'm grateful for the chance to make my ORAL potion. I'm grateful for the book Bastion gave me. I'm grateful for my health.* There, that was enough gratitude, especially when I was tired and cranky and not feeling grateful at all. Still, I *was* glad Mum was alive, and the book *was* really good.

Bastion came out of the bathroom, water droplets clinging to his tanned skin. Why on earth he couldn't remember to take his clothes *into* the bathroom I didn't know. I remembered easily enough. I pointedly draped my own clothes over my arm before stalking into shower. 'Be aggressive,' I chanted silently in my head. 'Be passive-aggressive!'

I drew on my protective runes before I dressed. The hot water had kick-started my bleary brain but I needed a coffee to get it fully operational. I checked the time: 6.15am. Yuck.

I looked at myself in the bathroom mirror and said my morning affirmations. 'It doesn't matter that you don't have a familiar even if Bastion does,' I said firmly this time, like I believed it. 'You are a strong, successful witch. You don't need anyone or anything.' Damn right.

I gave myself a brisk nod then headed out for my freshly squeezed orange juice. Okay, maybe I needed Oscar in my life. For a moment I imagined life without him and I swallowed hard. I missed Mum but if I lost Oscar too... I couldn't imagine it, *wouldn't* imagine it. He was my rock, the only person I could rely on.

I sent him a text. *Visit Mum this morning?*

Oscar is an early riser so his response was immediate. *Yes. 6.45 in the garage?*

Perfect, I replied. I wanted to add something emotional like *I love you* but I didn't. I have been emotionally crippled since my father abandoned me as a child. Hey, the first step in solving the problem is acknowledging you have a problem, right?

Mum was up and dressed. Her ferret, Lucille, was wrapped around her ankles, resting. They both looked old and it made me panic; Mum was too young to look so frail. I needed to look into potions or food supplements or *something*. I'd tried to heal her dementia so many times, but so far I hadn't succeeded. I refused to call it failure because I hadn't given up yet.

I added more work on Mum's potions to the never-ending to-do list and felt like I was drowning. I wished I had a sibling to share this burden but it was on me to look after her, and I was letting her down. I pushed aside the pity party and smiled.

She beamed back and the world righted itself for a moment. 'Hello, darling.'

My heart lifted. 'Hi, Mum.' I gave her a kiss.

'What's new with you?' she asked.

I considered what I could tell her. 'I'm working on a new potion.' I'd already told her that a hundred times but she forgot, so I kept on telling her. She was impressed every time, which was nice.

'Are you dear? What will it do?'

'Give us more time in the Other, I hope.'

'That would be marvellous, Am.' She leaned forward. 'That could change everything.' Her eyes gleamed with ambition. 'You'll go down in history. My little Amber, solving the biggest issue that the human side has.'

I smiled because her passion was fervent and real. She believed in me as she always had done. In the dark of the night the self-belief she'd instilled in me stoked my fire. I would succeed; of course I would. You could only fail if you stopped trying, and I would never do that. Failure wasn't in my vocabulary because my mum had deleted it.

Oscar moved a little, drawing her eye to him. 'Who are you?' she asked him, suddenly scowling. 'You look familiar.'

He smiled but it didn't reach his eyes. 'Just Amber's driver.'

'Well, there's no car here so you can get out.'

He ducked his head and turned to leave. As he did so, Mum spotted Bastion guarding the door. 'Bastion?' she called.

I froze. She knew Bastion?

Chapter 29

My mother was looking at Bastion, *seeing* him. 'Hello, Bastion. Is it time, then?' she asked, genuine curiosity lighting her tone.

'Perhaps,' he answered evenly. 'I'm guarding Amber.'

'As you have always done,' she noted approvingly.

'As much as I have been able. Some things I could not save her from.' I was surprised at the regret in his voice.

Mum, ever practical, waved that away. 'Hurt is a part of life – it moulds us, shapes us. How we deal with adversity defines us. You cannot wrap her in cotton wool any more than I could.'

'No,' Bastion agreed.

'What the heck are you two talking about?' I demanded.

'Is it time?' Mum asked again.

Bastion grimaced. 'Too much time, I think, Luna.' He looked at her pointedly and I knew I was missing half the conversation. The undercurrents were not meant for me.

She laughed and tossed her red hair that glittered with silver strands over her shoulder. 'I regret nothing.'

'No, you never did,' he replied ruefully. 'You were a stubborn child.'

'And now I'm a stubborn adult.' She winked at him before her expression grew serious. 'There is only forward motion, Bastion. Forward motion, Amber. Stagnation is the enemy. Help her.'

'You know that I will.'

Mum looked out of the window; when she looked back, she wasn't behind her eyes anymore. She smiled vaguely at Bastion and me and said politely, 'Hello, do I know you?'

My heart lurched. It was too fast; the lucidity had gone too quickly. I needed more time with her today and I wanted a hug from my mum. 'Not today,' I replied with a forced smile. 'Have a nice day.' I didn't add 'Mum' though I was desperate to. The word might have meant a lot to me but it would confuse and upset her, so I let it go.

Rune ruin! She'd been lucid and I'd wasted it, yattering on about a potion she'd been told about a hundred times. Frustration tore through me. It was incredibly hard to walk away, but I strode out of her room and closed the door behind me.

Bastion followed on my heels. Before I could say anything, he touched my shoulder and pulled me into his arms. 'What are you doing?' I said, holding myself stiffly, my voice muffled by his chest.

'You didn't get a hug from your mum so I'm giving you one instead.'

My throat ached and tears throbbed behind my eyelids. I was *not* crying because he was hugging me. In fact, I was *mad* at him because he knew my mother and he'd never told me. I pushed him away. 'What the heck was all that?' I rounded on him. 'You didn't tell me you knew my mum.'

'I've lived for two centuries. If I listed everyone I'd met, we'd be here all week,' he answered evasively, not meeting my eyes.

'I don't care about everyone, I care about Mum. How does she know you? What are you to her?'

His expression grew rueful. 'A friend, perhaps.'

I turned angrily to Oscar. 'You knew about this?' My eyes pleaded with him to deny it because I felt like the rug was being pulled out from under me. My mum knew Bastion, liked him, joked with him. He'd been my greatest enemy for months – I had *loathed* him – and now he was sleeping under my bed, buying me books and laughing with my mum? It made no sense.

'Yes, I knew that Bastion and Luna were friends,' Oscar admitted. 'That's what Bastion and I were arguing about last night. I wanted to tell you as much as we could.'

'As much as you could?' I parroted. 'Why can't you tell me everything?'

'Luna believed in oaths.' Oscar sighed. 'You know that.' It hurt so much that he used the past tense when we spoke of her, but today she hadn't known him and the human heart can only take so much. That reminder served like a bucket of iced water over my head and my anger drained away as quickly as it had risen.

I reached out and touched his arm. 'Sorry,' I said miserably. 'I'm sorry.' I wasn't sure quite what I was apologising for; Goddess, this was a mess.

Mum had done something, something that Bastion and Oscar were keeping from me. She'd mentioned a prophecy to me in the past, so maybe I needed to go to the Hall of Prophecy to see what I could learn. But not now; now I needed to focus on the black witch and the potion. I had to hope that, with those two things squared off, the attempts on my life would also stop. I would have time for Mum's mysteries later. I had a plan – I just had to stick to it.

I heard Mum's voice in my head, *Forward motion, Amber. Stagnation is the enemy.* Maybe it was, but so was whoever had me in their crosshairs. Forward motion wasn't enough. I needed to duck and dive to survive and at some point I would have to shoot back.

Chapter 30

After the disastrous visit to Mum, my day went from bad to worse when I got a call from Jeb. 'You'd better get back to the tower,' he said quietly. 'There's been another attack.'

Dread curled in my stomach. 'Who?' I demanded.

'Meredith's familiar, Cindy,' he whispered. 'She's dead.' Cindy was Meredith's tortoiseshell cat. She was beautiful and affectionate and often found in the common room. I'd liked her.

My stomach lurched again. To kill a familiar is an unthinkable sin, even for a black witch, because familiars are sacrosanct. We each have one familiar in our lifetime, and once that is gone there is never a replacement. In witch law, familiars are at one with the witch; we are so closely connected that our actions are inseparable. Poor Meredith.

'Rune ruin,' I cursed. 'I'm on my way.'

Jeb took a breath and hesitated. 'Kassandra is dealing with it but I thought you'd want to know.'

Damn right I did. I guessed that was why he was whispering. 'Thank you, Jeb.' I hung up. 'Cindy's dead,' I told Oscar. 'Get us to the tower. Now.'

Bastion swore darkly. 'How was she killed?'

'Jeb didn't say. Let's move.'

Our car careened through the traffic as we sped home. Home and death. Life was a mess these days, and I didn't know what it said about me that I was pleased Bastion was next to me. He was an assassin who knew death intimately and he'd have insights. I'd take every advantage I could to find the damned killer.

I found myself battling tears again, and wondered if someone had slipped me something because it was unlike me to have my emotions so close to the surface. But the death of a familiar was so shocking. They are bound to us; they live our whole lives with us, giving us strength, magic and comfort. In return they get an extended life. To tear asunder that almost holy bond between a witch and her familiar was... I couldn't find the words. Meredith was alone now, like me, and that wasn't something I'd wish on my worst enemy.

We parked and hurried into the tower. I went straight to the flat Meredith shared with Ria. Meredith's husband,

Grant, had divorced her when Ria was little; he was a weak witch and he'd struggled to accept his wife's brilliance. He'd found it intolerable not being the breadwinner and eventually he'd left. He'd moved to America but regularly rang and video-called Ria. Now Meredith didn't have a partner to comfort her as she experienced a grief unlike any other.

Melrose – Melly – her best friend in the coven was bone idle and vapid but her heart was in the right place. I sent her a message and asked her to come to Meredith's flat, then I took a deep breath and squared my shoulders. The front door was closed but unlocked and there were no signs of forced entry. I went inside.

The tang of blood hung on the air, an all-too familiar scent these days. I heard sobbing from Meredith's bedroom so I went into the lounge instead, where Cindy was laid out. What I saw made my eyes fill and I brought a hand to my mouth to stop a sob. Kind, sweet Cindy had been butchered; her entrails had been ripped out and were pouring from her, and her green eyes were wide and glassy. The thing that makes us alive – that unique spark that animates us – was gone. As was her tail. I looked around but I couldn't see it. No doubt it had been taken as a sick trophy.

I clenched my jaw and refused to let the tears fall. I'd known Cindy for more than twenty years and my heart ached as much as if I'd lost one of my witches. I knelt by her small body and stroked her head. Her fur was still so soft.

I took several deep breaths before I stood up. Bastion was so close behind me that I almost stumbled. His hand shot out and he caught me. 'Cindy's a cat?'

I suddenly realised that he hadn't heard Jeb's side of the call because Jeb had been whispering. Bastion had been expecting a witch's body.

'Yes, sorry, I didn't think. Cindy is Meredith's familiar. You probably don't know much about familiars...' I trailed off. Of course he knew about familiars – after all, he had one! – but maybe not what they meant to witches. 'Witches' familiars,' I amended. 'They're special, so special to a coven. They're cherished and loved, bound to their witch for their whole life. And now Meredith will be alone. It's just awful.'

I expected him to make a derisory comment, to tell me that Cindy was just a cat, but instead his eyes were soft and sympathetic. 'I'm sorry for your loss.'

'Not mine, Meredith's.'

'Yours, too. And the whole coven's.'

I nodded because he obviously understood. I took a deep breath and tried to steady myself. There was nothing to be done for Cindy. 'Can you … wrap her in something? We'll hold a funeral for her later.'

Bastion nodded. 'I will. Let me just clear the flat before I leave you.'

I pressed my lips into a thin line, but he was just doing his job. He checked all the rooms before giving me the all-clear, and I caught him giving Oscar a head tilt as an instruction to follow me.

The door to Meredith's bedroom was already open from Bastion's quick check inside. She and Ria were sobbing, inconsolable, and Kassandra was rubbing Meredith's back, looking sympathetic. Meredith raised her head and saw me. 'Mother,' she whispered.

I reached for her and she fell into my arms. 'I'm sorry,' I murmured, stroking her hair. Coven Mother is an odd role: leader, confidante and mother. Now I was stepping into the latter role as I comforted Meredith. I couldn't imagine the loss she was suffering. 'We'll find the black witch,' I promised, my tone harsh. 'I promise you that.'

Her sobbing increased as she clung to me and it was a long time before her tears stopped.

We had a cup of tea. We'd moved up to my flat whilst Jeb removed the carpet in Meredith's living room and cleared all hints of violence and Cindy's passing. I took a sip from my mug, emblazoned with *Of course I talk to myself, sometimes I need expert advice,* and wished I had a few more sensible mottos in my cupboard. Meredith was sipping from a mug that had an image of a smiling avocado in trainers saying '*Avocardio*', though that was better than the fanny mug that Bastion was sipping from. Ria hadn't touched her tea; maybe she had issues with sipping from a cup with said *I used to be a people person ... but people ruined it for me.* It was my all-time favourite; Jake had given it to me for my twenty-first birthday.

I cleared my throat and looked at Meredith. 'I know this is hard, but we need to talk about what happened.'

'I know,' she said quietly. 'It's okay.' She took a deep breath. 'It was awful. I was upstairs in the coven library when suddenly I felt a pain in my stomach. It was so painful it took my breath away, like I had appendicitis or something. But I knew it wasn't my pain. I reached out to my bond and the agony crashed through me.'

She bit her lip and closed her eyes against the tears that wanted to fall. 'Cindy was clear that I needed to stay away, that the danger wasn't gone. She couldn't see her attacker but she could sense that they were still there. She sent me her love.' Her voice broke.

Ria glared. 'And of course you ignored her warning and went straight to her.' Her eyes were red-rimmed from her tears; for all her bolshiness, she'd been heartbroken too.

'I did,' her mum admitted. 'As you would have done. When I arrived, the front door was open—'

'There were no signs of forced entry,' Bastion interrupted. 'Have you recently lost a key or lent one out?'

Meredith shook her head. Ria snorted. 'Mum believes in an open-door policy. We never lock the front door.'

'We're in the coven tower,' Meredith protested weakly. 'We're safe here.' A lot of the covens up and down the country took that approach, but I'd always encouraged my witches to lock their doors. It took mere moments to unfasten a lock but the home is sacred. Mum hadn't believed in an open-door policy at home, just at work; I embraced the latter and enforced the former. It was unfortunate that Meredith was old school and had spent a lot of her formative years in the Liverpool coven where the open-home policy was still encouraged.

Ria shook her head, disgust written on her features. I felt sorry for Meredith; not only had she lost her familiar but her teenage daughter wasn't showing empathy for her mother's plight. Kids.

'I'll send an email reminding everyone to lock their doors until this situation is resolved,' Kassandra interjected, pulling out her phone to do just that.

I nodded my permission for the coven-wide email, but it grated that she wasn't *asking* if she should do it. Sharing a role was harder than I'd expected because right now I didn't give a toss about my potion; I just wanted to find the perpetrator of this heinous crime and bring them to justice, one way or another.

'Can I suggest we work together on this?' I said tightly.

'Of course. Let's put together an action plan.' Kassandra paused and slid her eyes to Meredith and Ria. 'Later.'

I nodded: later, when we were alone. There was a knock at my door. Oscar opened it and Melrose flounced in. 'Merry!' she cried. 'My God! Merry! I'm so sorry.'

'Melly!' Meredith collapsed in tears again as her best friend barrelled in.

I grimaced as I noted that Melrose had her budgerigar familiar with her. Bringing Rocky hardly showed great sensitivity. He flew from Melrose's shoulder and settled on my coffee-table lamp.

I nodded towards my office; Kassandra and I could talk in there whilst the other three witches grieved together. Bastion rose as he saw my intention and once more directed Oscar. This time he told him to stay and watch over the three women whilst he watched over me and Kass.

I felt like I was being wrapped in cotton wool, but the stakes just kept on rising. Something had to give.

Chapter 31

I waited until we were all safely ensconced in my office before saying, 'We need a trap.'

'I love traps.' Kassandra grinned. 'What are you thinking?'

'We use the one thing black witches always want.'

'Pain and death?' Kassandra said dubiously.

'Power,' I corrected. 'We'll let it be known that in order for me to hunt down the black witch, I will carry out a power-boosting ceremony using one of the crystals in my office. A Himalayan crystal which, when used, temporarily amplifies a witch's powers.'

Kassandra looked impressed. 'I didn't know you owned a Himalayan crystal.'

'I don't,' I said drily. 'That's why it's a *trap*. Bastion, can you discreetly arrange cameras in my office that we can monitor?'

He nodded. 'I already have them installed.'

My eyes narrowed at the blatant invasion of my privacy. He hadn't told me he'd taken that step and it felt rude and invasive. He interpreted my glower correctly and held up his hands. 'I had them installed last night so that the coven would be none the wiser – bar the receptionist who let in my security man.'

'Who did you use?'

'Tom Smith. He was in the area doing a job for Emory, so rather than delegate he came himself.' I trusted Tom about as much as I trusted anyone, but I trusted Emory and his judgement more. I settled down. 'Okay. And what about my flat?'

'He's going to come by in,' Bastion checked his watch, 'half an hour to deck it out. I want a visible deterrent, so he'll check in with reception and march up and down telling everyone he meets that he's here to install security for you.'

I nodded begrudgingly. I didn't want another bedtime explosion.

'We're getting off track,' Kassandra pointed out. 'How are we going to disseminate the information about the crystal?'

'Simple. I'll tell Ria.' Kassandra stared at me, waiting for me to elaborate. 'Ria will tell her boyfriend, Henry, and her friend Sarah, who'll tell her mother Venice, who'll tell everyone she meets. Henry will tell his dads and before you know it, the whole coven will know.'

Kassandra laughed. 'It's not just my tower that's full of gossips, then?'

'No,' I groused, 'I think it comes with the territory. Witches just love to gossip and gab.'

'Who doesn't?'

Me, but I am weird in lots of ways. My business is my own, and I find the thought of the witches gossiping about Mum and her condition abhorrent. However, I am realistic enough to accept that it is a favourite pastime.

'We'll tell everyone that I'll do the ritual tomorrow at midnight when the moon is full. That will put the black witch under time pressure to do something stupid,' I said grimly. 'Obviously, no one outside of this room knows it's a setup.'

'Not even Oscar?' Bastion queried.

'I trust Oscar with everything in me, but there's no need to tell him or anyone else.' I was only telling Kassandra as a courtesy since she was acting Coven Mother, plus she'd arrived after the incident with Fehu's wings and the vampyr. I was almost certain she wasn't involved. If the black witch didn't enter my trap, I'd be taking a harder look at her; after all, she *had* been in the area the day before. She wasn't off the suspect list; she was just way down it.

'We keep this between ourselves,' I ordered. Kassandra nodded solemnly. 'All right then, let's put things in motion.'

When we returned to my living room, Tom Smith had arrived with a couple of other brethren and they were already assessing where to place cameras, motion detectors and other security equipment that was way beyond my skillset. I nodded to Tom and left them to it. My focus was on the three witches sitting on the sofa.

Meredith had calmed down and the storm of tears had passed. Melrose had an arm around her, and Ria was sitting close by looking miserable. Hopefully some gossip would cheer her up.

I cleared my throat and sat down. 'We've formulated a plan. I know an ancient ritual that will enable us to use Cindy's blood to help identify her killer.' It was complete BS, of course, but anything spoken with authority is easy to believe. Even lies.

'To carry out the ritual I need a power boost first because the ritual uses an extreme amount of magic to work. I have an ancient Himalayan crystal in my office, the tall pink one in my drawer. I'll use that to boost my power tomorrow, then I'll conduct the ritual under the light of the full moon. I promise we're going to find the black witch who killed Cindy – and any others in this tower.' At least my last statement was true; the rest of it would have had Jinx's lie detector ringing like a klaxon.

Not for the first time I wished that Jinx was with me. It would have been *so* much easier if she could have questioned all the witches in the tower. Wham bam, black witch, ma'am. Ironically, it was for that reason Jinx keeps her truth-seeking hidden – it would be too easy for someone to grab her and misuse her. She isn't anyone's tool, not even her friends'.

Ria was looking antsy. No doubt she was dying to spread the gossip already. 'It's a secret,' I added. 'Don't tell anyone. Not a single soul.' I fixed my eyes on her. 'Not even Sarah.' There, that would do it. By the end of the day everyone in the tower would know my plan.

Chapter 32

My phone rang: Tobias. I swiped to answer. 'Hello?'

'Amber DeLea, I have sourced the vervain for you.'

'Lavender golden wind vervain,' I specified. I could get blue vervain anywhere.

'Of course. But there is a … complication.'

Of course there was. 'What?'

'The grower insists he won't sell us anything if you don't meet with him. He's based in Liverpool.' Tobias's exasperation was clear.

I sighed. 'When?'

'Tonight.'

'I'm in Buckinghamshire,' I pointed out.

'The supplier will arrange a helicopter for you.'

Wonderful, another bloody helicopter ride. I hoped this one wouldn't end up with my blood in it. 'Fine. Send me an ETA of the helicopter once you know it.' I paused. 'Thank you.'

I hung up before he could reply and twirled a strand of my red hair whilst I thought it through. The stage was set here in the tower. I didn't need to monitor the cameras in the office because someone I trusted could do that – Oscar was the one that came to mind. Jeb was a close second but Oscar was the only one I knew I could trust without a shadow of a doubt. Firstly, he wasn't a witch, black, white or otherwise. Secondly, I'd known him most of my life and he was more of a father to me than my own dad had ever been. So, it would have to be Oscar. Then Bastion and I could go to Liverpool and meet this tricksy grower.

I met Bastion's eyes. They were watching me as they always seemed to be. 'Tobias's supplier won't give me the vervain without meeting me. He's in Liverpool so they're sending a helicopter.'

He scowled unhappily. 'It could be a trap.'

'Mr Glass-Half-Empty,' I bitched. 'I need the vervain. We've got just over twenty-four hours until we spring our trap on the black witch, so we might as well get this sorted.'

'Unless the black witch is springing a trap on *you.*'

I considered it. 'I don't think it's likely,' I said finally. 'Tobias has been one of my suppliers for years and he's never led me astray. Besides, if it is a trap I'll have you.'

'Flattering as your confidence in me is, I'm only one man.'

'Griffin,' I corrected. 'By the way, how are you doing with your deathly urges?'

He looked at me impassively. 'I have the urge to kill you right now.'

I shot back my own impassive glance. 'No you don't. You like me.'

He sighed and muttered almost inaudibly, 'I do.'

It was enough to make me freeze. He liked me? After all the crap I'd given him? I had virtually signed his death warrant by instructing the witches not to break the black witch's curse that had been on him, and my conscience twinged painfully. Not my finest moment. I was better than that. I wanted to be better than that.

To my surprise, when the helicopter arrived so did Fehu. He landed on my shoulder and looked pointedly at me and then at the helicopter. 'Um, does Fehu want to come with us?' I asked.

Bastion nodded. 'We need more eyes. He's volunteered.' I didn't point out that Fehu was a *bird*. He wouldn't be much of an asset if another ogre came strolling by with murder in mind. Still, it was Bastion's gig; I knew about healing people, potions and runes, he knew about killing things. Between us we had covered a lot of bases.

We climbed in. The pilot didn't comment on Fehu's presence. I guess when you fly for the Other realmers, you get used to crazy things happening. A bird probably barely registered on the weirdo-meter.

The pilot didn't require directions. He seemed to know exactly where he was going, which was good because someone needed to.

We landed in Liverpool just as darkness was descending. The lights twinkling over the city made it look beautiful and I wished we had time to stroll around the docks. Liverpool is one of my favourite places in the world and the thought of moving here if I became the Symposium member made me smile. Mum had brought me here for holidays; whilst other kids were going to Blackpool to see the lights, she was drilling me on the strengths, weaknesses and characteristics of different species.

We used to come here, away from the protection of the tower, so that I could learn more about the Other. Being a witch was all well and good, but I had to co-exist with more than witches. I'd spent many a happy hour in Tococo's coffee house and hall sipping baby cinos and eating blueberry muffins while we watched people come and pass through the portal. It was fascinating watching them go from human to suddenly having flames dancing on their heads, or their pale-pink skin change to the lurid purple complexion of a seer.

I looked down longingly as we passed over Lark Lane; the little street was one of my favourite places, full of independent cafes and restaurants and with an amazing potions' shoppe. Finally we landed in the huge space that is Sefton Park. By day this area of greenery is a hot spot for families and tourists in the middle of a glorious cosmopolitan city that I'd always loved.

'The Palm House,' the pilot grunted. Well, at least we knew where we were heading.

Chapter 33

I'd been to the Palm House before. It is a monumental greenhouse parked like a UFO in Sefton Park. The dome-shaped Victorian building is filled with lush flora and fauna. It should have come as no surprise that a dragon was the one who wanted to meet me in this verdant area.

As we started towards the Palm House, Bastion gave a low whistle and Fehu took to the skies to scout the path ahead. The place had long since closed to visitors and the tourists were gone for the day. At the entrance we were greeted by a pixie. She was just shy of a foot tall with butterfly wings the size of my hands. She wore a sage-green dress and had matching green skin, the same as the dryads.

'Hello,' I called as we approached. 'We're looking for a dragon.'

She sniffed disdainfully. 'You've kept Peter waiting long enough. He's in his glen. I'll take you to him.' She flew not towards the main entrance but to a small side entry that said 'Staff access only'. I guessed the pixie was staff because she pulled out a key and unlocked the door.

Bastion went to open it for her but I touched his arm to hold him back. Pixies are incredibly proud – and stubborn to boot. If she needed help she'd ask for it, but if Bastion opened the door for her in a gentlemanly manner she'd be hissing at us for the rest of the way.

Her little arms flexed as she pulled open the door; it was a struggle but she managed it then shot us a triumphant look. I kept my expression neutral but inwardly I gave her a little cheer; she'd gone for it, worked hard and got the result she needed. She was my kind of girl.

'This way,' she breezed, like it hadn't been a gargantuan effort. As we followed her down the corridors, I had to stop myself from reaching out and touching the plants around me, some of which I'd never even seen in real life. It was more than three years since I'd last been to the Palm House and even then I hadn't been behind the scenes like this; I'd been with the hoi polloi, a paying visitor like everyone else. It was clear that the team of growers had been busy since I'd last visited. The Common realmers who worked here had no idea that these pretty, exotic plants were hotbeds for potion ingredients.

I gasped suddenly as I spied black kiteen. Those dark purple leaves were worth more than my entire flat. They were incredibly rare and my coven had been trying to source them for at least the last year. I should have approached Tobias before, but we hadn't reached emergency stations – though perhaps we had now.

I swear the pixie took us the long route on purpose, winding this way and that so that I could gasp in delight at plant after plant that I would have given a limb to possess. Luckily, dragons don't like being paid in limbs or I'd have had nothing left.

Movement up ahead caught my eye, and I saw Fehu flying above us on the other side of the glass. He didn't look distressed so I took that to mean that there wasn't a battalion of ogres waiting up ahead.

No ogres, but an unassuming man with black hair and a neat pair of glasses who was beavering away in the soil. The glasses were an affectation because all dragons have perfect eyesight. He turned and rose when he heard our footsteps, dusting his filthy hands on his trousers. That made little difference; the hand that he extended towards me was still filthy. I blinked at it, not because of the dirt but because we don't shake hands in the Other. There are too many seers, empaths and wizards floating around who can use physical touch either to compel you or to gather information from you. No doubt that was this man's intention – but what information was he after?

I hesitated a beat too long and his youthful face drew down in a frown. Dammit, I needed that vervain, so I reached out and clasped his hand. He shook it then held it a moment longer. The moment became a minute and my skin prickled uncomfortably at his prolonged touch. Finally he smiled, flashing warm brown eyes at me. 'I had to be sure,' he murmured. 'Sorry for the intrusion.'

'Sure of what?'

'Your intentions.'

I frowned at him.

'I needed to know what you want to do with my plants,' he elaborated. 'Many of the ingredients here could do a great deal of damage in the wrong hands.'

'I know. I saw the black kiteen.' I tried to keep the wonder out of my voice but I suspect I failed miserably.

'Exactly. It can bring life if used sparingly, or death if you are heavy handed. And that's only one of my ingredients. There are thousands of others.'

Jeez, don't brag, Peter. 'It's your hoard,' I noted. This was a dragon that hoarded potion ingredients rather than wealth, although the one would surely lead to the other. If he was an indiscriminate seller, he was sitting on a hoard of millions.

'Indeed. I hoard potion ingredients, which is why I can't give them away willy-nilly. I need my hoard to sustain me – but I can part with a few ingredients.'

'For the right price,' I commented, a shade cynically.

'For the right cause,' he corrected sharply.

'And is my cause right enough for you?'

'To end the rift between the creatures and the humans?' He nodded solemnly. 'Yes. That is a worthy cause.'

Bastion's eyebrows shot up and I suddenly realised I had never described the purpose of my potion to him. On the surface, yes: it was simply to give the witches more time in the Other and free us from flitting back and forth to the portals. The portals help us access the Other, but once you've been in the magical realm, returning to the Common is a source of anxiety to many. The fact that the creatures don't have that same limitation and vulnerability has been a source of conflict for years. If I could remove that, perhaps the enmity between the two sides would disperse. It was worth trying, not just because my name would be remembered for the rest of time but because it was the right thing to do.

'What are you?' I asked Peter. To understand my intentions so clearly, he must have empathy or seer magic or *something*.

'A dragon,' he answered simply – and evasively – and went back to tending his plants. Dragons can't lie but they have no issue in omitting a tonne of information. 'You may go, Amber DeLea, and take your vervain with you.'

'Lavender golden wind vervain,' I specified, lest he try and foist me off with blue vervain. I cleared my throat. 'The black kiteen...'

He answered without turning. 'One leaf.'

'Thank you. Thank you so much,' I gushed.

'Marsha, if you would, give them containers for the ingredients.' His tone was gentle as he spoke to the pixie.

'Of course, Peter,' she hummed happily. She buzzed off and returned a few moments later with some Tupperware.

'And the price?' I asked reluctantly.

'That has been settled through Tobias. Your terms with him are what they are. My terms with him are what they are.'

'Yes, but the black kiteen is extra,' I pointed out. I am a woman of principle and I would never steal anything. Taking the ingredient without payment felt like I was bending my own rules.

He finally looked up. 'You will use it as it should be used?'

'Yes,' I swore fervently.

'Then it is a gift. A "buy one get one free" special. A BOGOFF. I don't often do those, but you did fly all this way so that I could shake your hand.'

I didn't point out that he had given me no choice. 'Thank you,' I repeated. 'If ever you have need of a witch, please call on me.' I stopped shy of formally recognising the debt, but he would recognise the inference just the same.

I pulled out one of my business cards from my voluminous skirt pockets and handed it to him. It had my personal number on it rather than coven's direct line. Peter pocketed it and turned to Bastion. 'Two steps behind her. No more, no less.'

Bastion blinked before giving the barest nod. He looked a moment longer at Peter, before he drew back and swept him a courtly bow. What the heck?

'Two steps,' Peter repeated. Then he turned his back on us again.

I followed Marsha down the winding corridors lined with greenery and Bastion stayed the prescribed two steps behind me. When Marsha stopped and pointed imperiously, I carefully harvested the selected potion ingredients and placed them in the containers.

She produced a small woven tote bag for me to put them in. The tote bag said *Become a tree hugger ... they can't run!* I wondered what the dryads would think of people coming and hugging their trees. Marsha seemed a little mischievous, so I could fully imagine she'd guide people to hug the *wrong* tree. Dryads are possessive and some of them carry knives; it is best not to upset the wrong one.

I shouldered the tote, almost preening at the feel of the ingredients close by. This was a coup of epic proportions; not only would the vervain enable me to complete the ORAL potion, but the black kiteen would make my coven, the much-derided *hula* coven, the first to produce more of the Last Defence potion in more than a decade. And now I knew where there was more black kiteen, I had a bargaining chip. A huge one.

Chapter 34

Marsha was done for the day. As night had well and truly descended, we offered to escort her back to her tree as we returned to the helicopter.

'Well, this is me,' the pixie said, when we reached a grove of willow trees. 'Good night.' A yawn cracked her little face.

She reached out and touched her tree in greeting before gasping and whirling around. 'Watch out!' she screeched in panic. Above us, Fehu cawed a warning and swooped down towards us, but he was too slow and Bastion ... Bastion wasn't two steps behind me.

A green-skinned arm reached out around my middle and yanked me backwards towards a tree. A dryad. At the same time as I saw the arm, a flash of light reflected off a blade that was swinging towards me.

Being grabbed from behind like that awoke the old instincts Mum had instilled in me. *Make a scene and*

SING; Solar plexus, Instep, Nose and Groin. I screamed loudly then slammed my right elbow as hard as I could into my attacker's solar plexus before I stamped with all of my might on his foot. As I flung back my head, I heard a satisfying crunch as I broke his nose.

Fehu dived down and his claws raked my attacker's face. The arm around me loosened but before I could complete the next manoeuvre – kicking him in the groin – I felt an agonising pain in my stomach. I stared down in disbelief at the knife that now protruded from my blouse. I had been *stabbed.*

I had seen a lot of wounds in my time as a healer but it was somewhat different when the wounds were your own. I touched the handle dumbly.

There was an animalistic screech of rage and I felt a warm spray of something splattering my neck and back. The coppery tang of blood scented the air, but I wasn't sure if it was mine or someone else's.

'Amber,' Bastion said urgently.

I looked up at him, but I felt sluggish and weird. Shock: I was probably in shock.

'Motherfucker!' he swore. Bastion was in human form but his eyes were shining gold instead of their usual black and his hands were taloned. Doing a partial shift is a very rare talent indeed; no wonder he was recognised as the paramount assassin of the griffin's guild.

Bastion let out a stream of swear words, some of which were amusingly inventive. 'I was four steps away,' he confessed, his voice strained. 'The bastard dryad came out of the damned tree.'

'Not the tree's fault,' I said mildly. I turned and looked at my attacker. The dryad's skin was dark green and it looked darker still in the depth of the night. His throat had been ripped out revealing his spinal column: C2, C3, and C4, I noted clinically. His hazel eyes stared at the canopy of trees above him, sightless and unmoving. Fehu's claws had done good work on his face and blood oozed from the claw marks. He was definitely dead.

'Amber,' Bastion said urgently. 'Are you okay?'

I turned back to him and wobbled a little. I guessed he hadn't seen the black handle of the knife protruding from my stomach. I gestured towards the offending area just as my legs failed me. He cursed violently as he caught me. He glared at the pixie and let out a low threatening growl. 'If you were involved in luring us here—'

'No! I swear!' she jabbered in fear. 'I had no idea Finnigan was here. I promise on my magic – may I lose it if I lie. So mote it be.'

'So mote it be,' I mumbled.

'She needs a healer,' Marsha pointed out urgently.

'No shit?' Bastion snarled back. 'If I find out you had anything to do with this, I'll rip your wings off and feed them to you.' Marsha sank back against her tree, eyes wide and teeth clacking with fear.

I was vaguely shocked by his threat. Despite the fact that he was a stone-cold killer, I'd never seen him so ... scary.

Bastion lifted me into his arms. I barely had time to register that my precious tote bag was still on my shoulder before he started running towards the helicopter. Despite his speed he hardly jostled me, which was good because the knife was still very much embedded in me. Bastion knew enough about healing – or perhaps killing – to leave it in. The blade was acting as a plug, stemming the broken blood vessels, stopping me from bleeding out. I was stabbed, I was in pain, but I wasn't in danger whilst the knife remained.

It seemed to take no time at all to reach the helicopter. 'Where is the nearest healer?' Bastion asked me urgently. He tapped my cheek lightly. 'Amber, stay with me. Where do we take you?'

'Liverpool coven. Jasmine,' I managed to say. Time was moving strangely, and I definitely wasn't playing with the Third realm. I only seemed to blink and Bastion was carrying me out of the helicopter again.

I realised that I was slipping in and out of consciousness. I was cradled in his arms and he was warm and smelled nice, a comforting scent ... sandalwood? And something else ... rosemary? A hint of something relaxing, maybe lavender? Perhaps that was why I felt safe even though I was in agony. It was definitely the lavender, I thought sleepily.

Bastion was shouting. Joe, one of the concierges, rushed us to the lifts. It wouldn't do for him to see me drifting. 'Hi, Joe,' I managed.

'Miss DeLea,' he responded, eyeing me with concern.

'How is Caroline?' I asked after his wife.

'She's fine, thank you.'

'Good.'

It would have worked better if I hadn't been slurring a little, but it was better than nothing. I had nothing if I didn't have my dignity, so I clung to consciousness with all my might. Passing out isn't on the cards, I told myself firmly.

The lift dinged and the doors opened. Joe rushed out and banged on Leanne and Jasmine's door. 'Shush, not so loud,' I chastened. 'You'll wake Jade.' I have a soft spot for Jade Melia, a young witch who had lost her parents when she was entirely too young. Leanne and Jasmine had adopted her, but it had been a rocky start for them all. By all accounts Jade was settling in, something I credited to Jinx. My friend had definitely done or said something to her, but both of them had been tight lipped about it. I suspected rules had been broken but, on that occasion, I was happy to let it slide.

Jasmine opened the door with Leanne behind her, pulling on a dressing gown. Jasmine was beautiful even in the middle of the night. Her inky-black hair, poker straight from her Chinese heritage, always gleams like she has just brushed it. Her eyes were clear and focused with not a hint of sleepiness. That boded well for my survival, I thought cheerfully.

'Bring her in here,' she ordered Bastion, gesturing to what I knew was their bedroom.

I was laid gently on top of the duvet. 'The blood will ruin your sheets,' I protested mildly.

'We'll buy new ones,' Leanne said calmly. 'Don't fuss, Mother.' The younger woman gently pressed my shoulder, encouraging me to lie back on their bed. They had good sheets; I wondered what the thread count was.

'I'm not *your* Coven Mother,' I noted, though I'm not sure why my brain felt like that was an important distinction.

'You're still *a* Coven Mother – and if the rumours are true, soon you'll be more.'

'Rumours are like mushrooms. They grow in the dark, ignorant of small things like truth,' I muttered.

Leanne laughed. 'Even when you're bleeding out, you're still dispensing wisdom.'

'It's one of the burdens of being so smart,' I sassed, making her snicker again.

Jasmine had retrieved pots of potions. I recognised them, of course, and tried not to feel apprehensive about the next part of the process. She couldn't heal me with the knife inside me but pulling it out wasn't going to be pleasant. I'd done it plenty of times to others and I'd heard the screams and the crying. I wasn't keen on being on the receiving end.

'Does it have to come out?' I whined.

'You know it does,' Jasmine answered evenly. She nodded to Bastion. 'Can you pull it out?'

He shook his head. 'I'd rather not. I don't want to cause her more pain. Can one of you do it?'

'I will,' Leanne offered. 'I've done it plenty of times before. Ready, Jaz?'

Jasmine nodded, a paintbrush liberally smeared with healing potion already in her hand. I braced myself and Bastion turned away. Leanne grasped the hilt of the knife and pulled.

I screamed.

Chapter 35

Jasmine was quick with her paintbrush, but I still ruined their bedsheets with my blood. I made a mental note to send them the money for a new duvet and a cover set. Then I thought about the possible thread count of such luxurious bedding and added a little more.

Leanne and Jasmine wanted me to sleep in their bed but I declined and made my way to the penthouse suite; I'd used it plenty of times before and it felt almost like a second home. I hoped that one day it might be my permanent residence, though I felt a pang of regret; I'd miss the hula coven if I moved here permanently. I'd even miss Venice and Sarah and their gossiping.

Bastion was silent as we went upstairs. He was often quiet but now he was soundless – though he was vibrating with fury. I hoped he could contain it, at least until we were in the flat.

I flicked on the lights in the penthouse, then touched the wall to check the wards were on. They were newly painted and vibrating with energy: perfect. I went to close the curtains and paused to enjoy the view. The Liverpool coven is housed in an apartment building on The Strand and I could see the glitter of moonlight on the water and the vibrant, red-brick docks.

There was a movement and I instantly recognised Fehu against the midnight sky. I opened the window so he could come in and join us. As he flew to my side, he gave a *kraa* of distress. He nuzzled into my neck before starting to fuss with my hair. He was anxious, so I took the time to give him a reassuring stroke or two. When he was calmer, I turned back to the stunning view and reluctantly closed the curtains. A yawn caught me off guard.

'We should eat before we sleep,' Bastion said tightly.

I looked at him. His jaw was tight and there was tension in every line in his body. I was tired and hungry and fresh out of diplomacy. 'What's eating you?' I asked irritably.

'You were just stabbed,' he said flatly.

'I'm fine.' I waved it away.

'I've been hired to protect you, Amber,' Bastion snarled. 'I failed you!'

Fehu let out a derisory *kraa*. He disagreed with Bastion, too. 'No, you didn't,' I argued. 'You killed my assassin and saved me. I'm alive. What else could you have done?'

'If I had stayed two steps behind you, you wouldn't have been stabbed,' he glowered.

This is one of the reasons that I hate dabbling with the seers. Knowing prophecies, knowing potential futures, always causes problems. Knowing a prophecy changes how you act and it becomes self-fulfilling. Keep me ignorant any day of the week and let my choices be my own. That was the main reason I hadn't visited the Hall of Prophecy despite Mum referring to a prophecy several times. Ignorance is bliss – isn't it?

'We don't know that Peter was right,' I dissented. 'Maybe he just meant a general warning to stay close.' Yeah, right; even I didn't believe that.

I pushed Bastion's concerns aside and rifled through the kitchen cupboards for some quick, easy food. I found some tins of soup and put them on the kitchen counter. Not exciting, but they would do. 'Soup?' I called to Bastion.

He grimaced with distaste at the tins. 'I'll sort food. You grab a shower.' Tactfully, he didn't point out that I was still covered in my own blood, and probably rather a lot of the assassin's too.

Fehu gave me one last snuggle before he left my shoulder to join Bastion, and I watched as he gave the griffin a little nuzzle. No doubt Bastion needed some comfort too. I guessed he was feeling bad about failing a mission, even though I disagreed with his assessment.

I didn't argue. Now that he'd reminded me, the stench of blood was making my nose recoil. I smelled like wet pennies. I went into the master suite for a shower, leaving the boys to have some bonding time.

I left my dirty clothes in a pile on the bedroom floor before I stepped into a scaldingly hot shower. I scrubbed my body, paying particular attention to my stomach where there should have been a scar. Jasmine was so good that there wasn't the slightest trace that I'd been injured a short time before.

A wave of tiredness rolled over me. Healed or not, blood loss was still a thing. Jasmine hadn't had a hydration potion and the potions store was locked for the night. I would have to deal with it the old-fashioned way. I slid down the shower and sat as a wave of dizziness swept over me. I thought of a cup of tea with longing, then let the hot water pour over me as I rested my head against the cubicle wall.

When I felt a little less wobbly, I stood up, shut off the water and swayed my way out. I wrapped the towel around myself for modesty's sake and entered the bedroom. Silk pyjamas were laid out for me on the bed and my dirty, bloody clothes had been removed – by Bastion, no doubt.

I slid on the pyjamas, but I was still feeling a little cold so I shrugged into the bathrobe hanging behind the door. Feeling warmer and less vulnerable, I left the bedroom, my damp red hair trailing down my back.

I inhaled as I walked into the open-plan space that was the twin of my own flat. My stomach let out an appreciative rumble: steak. Bastion was just serving up. 'I've done your steak rare for now. Do you want it medium or well done? I can cook it for longer.' He looked oddly domesticated, standing in a kitchen clutching a pair of tongs.

'No, rare is great. Thanks,' I said awkwardly. Where the heck had he found steak?

The steak was served with puy lentils, chips, wilted spinach and broccoli. Virtually the whole meal was designed to help me recover from blood loss, complete with a glass of orange juice to help me absorb the iron.

I almost inhaled my food and Bastion did the same. It had been far too long since our last meal – and that hadn't been a satisfying one – so this one hit the spot. When I'd finished eating, Bastion wordlessly flicked on the kettle, made us a brew and brought over a blueberry muffin. My eyes lit up at the sight of my favourite dessert; I couldn't have stopped my smile if I'd tried. 'How did you do all this?' I waved at the empty plates.

'I know people,' he answered evasively.

'*I* know people but I couldn't have put this together at—' I checked the time '—11pm.'

'I know people and I'm rich,' he added.

I gave a wry smile. He was right: money talks. He'd greased palms to get me steak.

'Thanks, anyway,' I muttered again. 'I'm going to bed. I'm exhausted.'

He rose with me and we took turns using the bathroom. I turned off the bedroom light, slid beneath the sheet and closed my eyes. I heard Bastion tug a pillow off the bed. 'You don't need to do that here,' I blurted out. 'No one has tried to bomb me in my sleep here.' It was illogical but true; I felt *safe* here. No need to make Bastion sleep on a hard wooden floor. We were adults; we could share a double bed.

I paused. 'Just ... just check under the bed first, okay?' My voice sounded small and embarrassed; I was glad the light was off so he couldn't see the heat rising in my cheeks.

He said nothing but grabbed his phone from the bedside table, flicked on the torch and looked under the bed. Then he crawled underneath and checked even more thoroughly. When he crawled back out, he shone the torchlight in a few other places, checked the lampshade, the drawers and the cupboards. Finally, he double-checked the window was secure before clicking off the torch.

He set his phone back down. 'All clear,' he promised calmly, no trace of mockery in his voice. He stood at the foot of the bed. 'Are you sure you're okay to share the bed with me?'

Absolutely not. 'Of course. We're adults. It's fine. Get in,' I said firmly.

He slid in next to me, careful not to touch my skin. He was wearing his usual teeny-tiny boxer shorts and nothing else. His scent was strong in the air; he'd just showered and the sandalwood washed over me. It was a nice smell and it was the only reason I was feeling ... weird. It was odd to share a bed, that was all. I hadn't shared a bed in at least a decade, platonically or otherwise.

'Goodnight, Sebastian,' I said finally.

'It's just Bastion,' he corrected.

Huh. 'I assumed that you'd dropped the Seb.'

'No. It's just Bastion.'

'As in a stronghold that gives protection?'

'Yes.'

That was oddly fitting, considering his current role in my life. 'Why did your father name you that?' It seemed weird to name any griffin something that meant protection. There was a long pause and I worried that I'd inadvertently offended him. Maybe his father had been absent like mine.

'The seers name us for something important that's going to happen in our lives,' he said finally.

I felt like I was in dangerous territory so I sought a way to segue the conversation. 'What does Shirdal's name mean?' I asked curiously.

'The meaning behind our names is considered very private, but Shirdal's is common knowledge so I'll tell you. *Shirdal* means griffin in Persian, and there the *shirdal* is a symbol of leadership.'

'Because he was going to become the leader of the guild,' I breathed. I felt rather than saw Bastion's nod.

The seers had been interfering again. I wondered what my name would have been if my destiny had been divined at birth. What would be my greatest contribution to the Other? What would I do to make myself proud?

Bastion's breathing evened out seconds after our conversation on names while my brain went on whirring. Thoughts tumbled in the confines of my skull. I was exhausted and I knew I needed sleep; after all, the next day we would spring the trap on the black witch. I'd need all of my wits about me to survive the coming confrontation.

Chapter 36

I awoke warm and relaxed – I hadn't had such a good sleep in years. I was rejuvenated in a way that I couldn't recall experiencing before. It felt glorious – until I realised that at least fifty percent of my warmth was borrowed.

I was plastered onto Bastion like fake tan on a Scouser. I couldn't move too suddenly or I'd wake him; how could I extricate myself without embarrassing the heck out of both of us? I was supposed to hate him and here I was pressed up against him like cheese against a grater. The analogy felt apt: he was sharp and could cut me with no effort at all, and I was fattening and liable to give you a heart attack.

I was still stuck on top of him when his breathing changed. 'Good morning, Amber,' he said calmly.

'Yup,' I squeaked. I rolled off like he was burning me and ran to the bathroom. I didn't need a shower but I decided to take one anyway. Hopefully, by the time I'd finished, my absolute mortification would have gone down the drain with the water.

Bastion wasn't in the bedroom when I stepped out, so I dressed in the clothes that he had helpfully laid out. Somehow he'd found a black skirt in my usual style – complete with pockets – and a vibrant green shirt. I suspected he had greased more palms but nevertheless I pulled them on gratefully.

I left my hair loose to dry as I said my affirmations into the mirror. I had no potions with which to paint on protective runes and I felt oddly naked without them, even though I was fully dressed.

I could smell something cooking. I went into the living area, then stopped and stared as Bastion flipped a pancake in the air. He was playing music and his hips were swaying. 'Bananas and cream or blueberries and cinnamon?' he asked without turning around. Did the man have eyes in the back of his head?

'Blueberries, please.' Did he even have to ask?

He plated the pancake, dusted it with cinnamon and sugar before adding chopped blueberries, then folded it in half and held it out to me. 'Here.'

'Thank you.'

I took my plate over to the table where a cup of tea awaited me. He'd even made it to my exact tea-colour preference; he was nothing if not observant. I drank the brew gratefully before diving into the pancake. It was utterly delicious, and I wondered why I didn't make them more regularly. After I had finished, another was ready for me.

Bastion made a further pancake while I wolfed my second one down. He turned down the music and put his plate and his own cooling cup of tea down on the table opposite me. 'Another pancake?' he offered, holding the third one out to me.

'No, thank you. You go ahead.'

He gave me a small smile and started to eat the last pancake. I watched him, frowning slightly. Bastion was feeding me pancakes before he'd eaten his own but he was my bodyguard, not my chef. I couldn't help feeling that I was missing something and it made me uneasy. Still, I wasn't one to look a gift pancake in the mouth.

I was feeling much better, no dizziness or any other side effects from my stabbing. Even so, taking a hydration potion would be sensible and I resolved to get one as soon as the potions store opened.

Bastion took the dirty frying pan to the sink and started to wash up. I watched, mesmerised. He hadn't even finished his pancake and he was *doing dishes*. What manner of man was he?

There was a knock at the door. As Bastion strode over to it, one of his hands shifted into talons; the other remained human so he could turn the door handle. The control that he had over his shift was astounding – I'd never seen anything like it.

He peered through the peephole. 'Jasmine,' he confirmed in a low voice.

'Let her in.'

His right hand returned to normal. If Jasmine had wanted to do me harm, she could have refused to open her door to me last night or somehow messed up the healing runes.

Bastion opened the door and she stepped in. She'd obviously made an effort with her appearance and taken the time to curl her hair. Mum taught me that it is rude to ignore it when someone makes an effort so I commented, 'Your hair looks lovely.' It really did, though I preferred it straight; I often think that our faces suit our hair the way it grows naturally. My hair looks weird when it is straightened and I think the waves suit the shape of my face.

'Thank you. It's something I do to de-stress.' She checked me over anxiously. 'Are you okay? Any lasting issues? Any pain?'

'She was dizzy yesterday when she was in the shower,' Bastion answered for me as he sat down again.

I glared at him. 'I've been fine since you cooked me that steak.'

Jasmine smiled. 'Great, a steak is ideal for low iron. Here, I've brought a hydration potion from the stores for you.'

'Thank you.' I took the vial from her, un-stoppered it and swallowed it in one, grimacing at the foul taste. Without speaking, Bastion cut a small corner of his pancake and held it to me on his fork. I don't love cream, but I hated the taste of the potion more so I leaned forward and ate it. Anything was better than that. It was surprisingly tasty; it seemed that bananas and cream was a good combination after all.

Jasmine was wringing her hands. 'I'm fine,' I reassured her.

'Oh, I know. That's not why I'm anxious.'

'Oh.' I coloured slightly at how self-involved I must have sounded. A thought occurred, sending a sharp lance of concern through me. 'Is Jade okay?'

She flashed a smile. 'She's fine – she's baking with Leanne. Erm, no, it's the potion store. Leanne often gets my potions for me, so it's been a while since I went down there. There are hardly any hydration potions left – and none of the missing ones were accounted for in the potions logs.'

'Oh for—' I stopped myself before an expletive slipped out, but my nostrils flared and I inhaled sharply. The hydration potion is multifaceted; it will help you if you are dangerously dehydrated or if you've lost too much blood. Someone was using the potion for the same purpose as me, blood recovery, and the only reason the withdrawals hadn't been noted in the log was because they were being used for nefarious purposes. In all likelihood, that meant we had another black witch using blood magic, this time in the Liverpool coven. Jasmine had obviously reached the same conclusion.

'How much do you trust Kassandra Scholes?' I asked grimly.

She blinked. 'I trust her absolutely.'

'There is evidence of a black witch operating out of my coven too. Kassandra officially arrived after the attacks started but she was already in the area.' Plus, it would be *so* much better if there was only one black witch – and not one of *mine.*

Jasmine shook her head slowly. 'No, I'm sorry, I can't believe it's Kass. She's kind and warm and nurturing. She actively helps the younger ones and revels in her role as a teacher, moulding young minds.'

'But to what path?' I demanded.

'The right one,' she responded sharply. 'I have never seen her use bloodletting, not even when it was the easiest solution.'

I had used bloodletting a time or two. I had no issue with the process itself; the problem wasn't the blood but the pain that came with it. Most consider bloodletting a bit of a grey area, but it's not black-witch territory. Sure, using blood is a rung on the ladder to evil, but it is using pain and death that really kick you down the well.

The missing hydration potions showed that someone was routinely using bloodletting either for themselves or a third party. Black witches use blood magic first and foremost because it allows them to fly under the radar for longer. Dead bodies equal questions and scrutiny; far better to kidnap someone, torture them and cause pain and injury. Use all of that pain to fuel some powerful spells then heal them and give them a hydration potion. You can then get a friendly subterfuge wizard to come and wipe their memories. Bing-bang-bosh: the victim thinks they lost track of time due to a heavy binge-drinking session with friends, *et voilà*. An almost victimless crime – apart from the victim, of course.

The potions' logbook was spelled so that false entries couldn't be entered; that meant that thieves simply omitted noting that they'd taken the potions. Dammit, there were supposed to be checks in place to stop that sort of thing.

Citing Kassandra as the black witch was the easy solution but my gut didn't like it. I didn't want there to be a black witch in my coven, let alone one in Liverpool, too. One black witch and an acolyte was bad enough; three was unthinkable.

Chapter 37

I instructed Jasmine to keep her suspicions to herself, not even to tell Leanne about her fears, and I assured her that I would discuss the matter with Kassandra. Jasmine said that I could trust all of the senior witches in the Liverpool coven – but we'd all thought we could trust Amelia Jane until she'd helped someone open a portal to a daemon dimension. Lesson learned. My trust has always been hard won and since then it had been virtually impossible to attain. Luckily Jinx and Lucy had sneaked into my heart before it had crusted over completely.

Bastion and I left Liverpool under a cloud of worry. I would have to speak to Kassandra about our suspicions but I'd make sure she was sitting on my truth-runed office chair before I did that. Fool me once and all that.

The helicopter ride back was silent. Fehu was conspicuously absent. 'Where's Fehu?' I asked Bastion when the silence became oppressive.

'He's flying under wing power. He didn't enjoy being in the helicopter – it was too noisy.' Fair point; the little avian hadn't had mini ear-defenders. 'He'll be back sooner than you think. He's a strong flyer.' There was a hint of affection in his voice that was so rarely present it surprised me. That was not to say that he didn't feel affection, but it was rare for him to display it.

When we touched down on the roof, I ran straight to my office and then into my hidden potions lab. I needed to secure the ingredients, pronto. I had already prepared the bell jars by painting them with *isa* for stasis, *algiz* for protection and *sowilo* for health and vitality. The three-rune combination would keep the ingredients in tip-top condition until they were ready to be used. Tension drained out of me as both ingredients were safely ensconced on my shelves.

I eyed the potion base in the cauldron. There was no reason to delay making the final version now I had the vervain as well as the kelpie water. I had all the ingredients, rare and otherwise, and I had my theory, so there was no time like the present. Except that there was a black witch floating around.

I gnawed my lip as I deliberated. No, I couldn't wait; someone was trying to kill me to prevent me from making this potion. I needed to succeed because it could be a game changer for so many – me included. Besides, the trap for the black witch was already in place; twiddling my thumbs wouldn't add to it.

Bastion was already at a laptop, remotely logging into the security feeds coming from my coven office. Oscar had been monitoring them but perhaps Bastion was as bad at delegation as I was. 'It's going to take a while to watch all of that,' I commented.

'I'll watch it at double speed and only when the cameras detect motion,' he explained.

'Double-checking Oscar's work?'

He shrugged. 'I trust him, but people make mistakes.'

'You trust him?' I said, surprised.

Bastion nodded, eyes still on the footage. I supposed it made sense – if he knew my mum, he also knew Oscar – but I'd never detected much camaraderie between the men. Was it because none existed or because they were keeping their friendship under wraps? The more I learned about Bastion, the more questions I had.

'I'm getting changed,' I said abruptly. In my newly decorated bedroom I pulled on some leggings that I'd asked Oscar to buy for me. I loved the image of him wandering around Primark picking out my clothes, though in reality he'd almost certainly sent one of the younger witches to do the shopping – Sarah or Ria, probably.

I pulled on a tank top and shirt. Dressed in clothes more suited to potion making, I went back to my lab. I was heating up the base to the right temperature when Bastion strolled in with his laptop in hand. 'Anything?' I asked hopefully.

He shook his head, his lips set in a grim line. If our trap wasn't attractive enough to the black witch, we'd have to resort to other methods. Grimmy would no doubt have one or two other options, but I wasn't keen on using him and bartering away weeks of my life in exchange for some ancient, long-forgotten spell work. The distinction between white and black witches wasn't so clearly defined in my ancestors' time, and some of them clearly hadn't given two figs about the difference. My ancestry was peppered with witches determined to change our world, some by means fair and others by means foul.

It was still early afternoon, so I had time to finish the potion *and* prepare for the black witch. I hoped the culprit would try to snatch the crystal from my office, but if that didn't work I'd go through a whole fake ritual at midnight and hope to be 'accidentally interrupted' by someone.

In the meantime, I needed to focus. I had everything I needed for success but I was so excited that I risked making a mistake. I took a deep calming breath. I could make the Other Realm Additional Length potion today, and it could be tested and in people's hands within a week. I could have the contract on me called off and Bastion banished from my life. I wondered why I felt uneasy at that last thought; maybe it was because I was too used to danger to accept that it would truly be gone. That was all.

Bastion's laptop was showing the cameras in my office. The screen was split so he could scan all four vantage points and his eyes were glued to the screen; how he didn't want to rip them out from sheer boredom was beyond me. I put him out of my mind and focused on the ORAL potion.

I chopped and minced. I ground and diced. I weighed and weighed again. *Measure twice, cut once*. I took notes of every step. I *knew* I was doing it correctly – I could feel the magical potential of the potion as it bubbled away. I added each ingredient separately, stirring until it was combined before I added the next. There were literally thousands of pounds' worth of ingredients in my cauldron; one misstep and it would all be wasted.

I checked the temperature, turned the gas down a little and tested the temperature again. We were at optimum combining temperature, so I added the kelpie water and waited with bated breath. The mist rolled off of the cauldron and the scent of ocean spray filled the room, despite the fact that the kelpie we'd taken the water from had been in a river. I stirred until my arms ached and the mist stopped rolling.

I was sweating and I took a moment to dab myself dry and remove my shirt. It wouldn't do to drip sweat into the cauldron. My hair was coming loose, so I stepped away and undid my braid then retied it and tucked in the loose strands. I rolled the braid into a bun and secured it with bobby pins. I didn't want to contaminate the potion with my hair, either.

It was time for the lavender golden wind vervain. Anticipation hummed through me and I gave myself a stern reminder not to get lost in flights of fancy. I plucked the leaves of the vervain and discarded the woody stems then sliced the selected leaves into thin strips. I checked the temperature again, tweaking it slightly to bring it back up after the cooling kelpie waters. I tested and tested again. When I was happy, I took a deep breath and added the sliced vervain leaves.

The potion crackled and bubbled violently. I watched breathlessly as it flashed gold once before it swirled and settled into a glorious lavender colour, the same colour as the skies in the Other.

Hope blossomed in my chest. It was perfect – it *had* to be perfect. I turned off the flame and started to stir, stirring for half an hour as the potion slowly cooled. Finally I tested the temperature again and assessed that it was cool enough to be placed in stasis. I covered the cauldron with its metal lid and painted on *isa* for stasis, *algiz* for protection and *sowilo* for health and vitality.

For good or ill, the ORAL potion was complete. Now the question remained – would it work?

Chapter 38

I was drenched in sweat and no doubt my cheeks were red and my hair bedraggled. I must have been in a complete state because Bastion was looking at me oddly. He cleared his throat. 'How will you know whether it works?' He nodded at the potion.

'I'll get the ORAL potion tested.'

There was a pause. 'Your *ORAL* potion?' His voice was incredulous.

'Yes.' Why was that so ridiculous?

His lips twitched. 'Don't you think that the name is going to cause – some confusion as to its purpose?'

'No, of course not. It's just an acronym for a potion that provides the user with Other Realm Additional Length,' I explained.

His lips twitched. 'Sure, but don't you think *that* will be confusing?'

I frowned. Did he mean people might think it was something to do with teeth? 'It's not like I'm making a potion for dentistry.'

He met my eyes and there was a heat there that surprised me. 'Not that type of oral,' he drew out.

'What other types of... Oh.' The penny dropped.

'Oh,' he repeated, a smile tugging at his lips.

I flushed. Oral *sex*. Right. Well. I clearly hadn't had that in a million years, since I hadn't even thought about it for a moment. My flush deepened as I recalled that ORAL was written on all the paperwork I'd submitted to the coven council, including the original grant request. How embarrassing. I pinched the bridge of my nose. 'Couldn't you have pointed this out earlier?'

'I didn't know earlier.' He shrugged. 'Otherwise I would have.'

I groaned and put my head in my hands as I thought about all the times I'd scrawled ORAL. *Everyone* must have been snickering.

'You could rename it,' Bastion suggested. 'The Other Realm Extender Potion. ORE.'

'That would be better,' I agreed, 'but the patent has already been filed. If this works, I'm going to be the witch that goes down in history for creating ORAL.'

Bastion lost it then. He threw his head back and laughed uproariously until a tear slid down his cheek. Despite my mortification, I found myself smiling. I'd never heard him laugh properly before, had never thought him capable of laughing like this because he was so contained, so reserved. I felt privileged to see him let loose. It meant something; if I'd had a moment to dig into what that was, I might have been in trouble.

When he calmed down, the grin remained. 'So how does it get tested? Swallowing a vial full of experimental potion seems a bit foolhardy.'

'A sure way for a potion maker to get dead,' I agreed. 'For every potion that works, there are another ten that have failed. Most successful potions take a huge amount of trial and error.'

'Do you think this one will work?'

I smiled with satisfaction. 'Yes, I do. I've spent years on this theory, extrapolating the perfect potion ingredients. This is my first practical experiment because of the difficulty and expense in procuring some of the ingredients. But yes, I believe it's going to work so the next step is getting it tested.'

'And how do you do that?' he asked again.

'I give it to the seers.'

'You get a seer to test your potion?'

'Why do you sound like you think that's ludicrous?'

'It's hardly scientific.'

I laughed. 'This isn't *science*, Bastion, it's *magic*.' My phone rang, wrenching my attention away from my protector. I swiped to answer. 'DeLea.'

'Miss DeLea.' I recognised Lord Wokeshire's refined tones immediately.

'Wokeshire. Have you managed to find the vampyr that cut off the imp's tail?'

There was a pause. 'He has been identified but not apprehended,' he said finally. 'We are working on taking him into custody. That is not the purpose of the call. The treatment that you have given my vampyrs is nearly complete and I'm pleased to report that the necromancer's hold has been broken.'

'I'm glad to hear that, but you must make sure they stay in isolation until they've finished the remaining vials,' I advised.

'Of course. We are following your instructions to the letter.' He cleared his throat. 'One of them managed to see the witch that stabbed him.'

Anticipation lanced through me. 'I can scry the witch from his mind.'

'Only once the hold is perfectly destroyed and touch is possible again. However, I did not wish for there to be any further delay in identifying the black witch so I engaged the services of a sketch artist who works with the police.'

'You have an image.'

'We do.' He sounded grim.

My phone vibrated. 'One moment.' I drew it away from my ear and clicked on the picture he'd sent me. It downloaded slowly. When I opened it, my jaw dropped. 'That can't be right,' I protested.

'You know her?'

I swallowed. 'I do.'

'The Red Guard will want to intercede.'

'No,' I said firmly. The Red Guard would kill her. 'This is coven business.'

'She tried to seize our vampyrs.'

'She will be dealt with appropriately by the coven council and the Connection.'

There was a long pause. 'I owe you, so I will give you twenty-four hours. After that, I must turn over what I have to the Red Guard.'

'I appreciate that,' I said evenly.

'Don't make me regret it.' He hung up, leaving me feeling lost. What had she been thinking?

Chapter 39

I lowered my phone from my ear slowly. Bastion was motioning urgently at me. 'We've got something,' he said grimly.

I put my phone on the workbench and turned to the laptop. When I saw who had crept into my office, I sighed softly. The vampyrs were on the money. We watched as Ria searched in my desk drawers for the 'Himalayan crystal'. She found the pink crystal, shoved it into a bag and left.

Bastion was watching my reaction. 'You're not surprised.'

'No. The potion I made released the vampyrs from her hold. One of them had seen her and Wokeshire arranged for him to work with a sketch artist.' I picked up my phone, unlocked it and swiped to the picture. Ria's face was sketched in pencil; it wasn't perfect, but it was unmistakably her.

Dammit, I'd really wanted it to be Briony or Timothy, someone I didn't think was an asset. Ria was young and she'd struggled a lot to find her place, but I'd hoped her relationship with Henry would settle her. It had been hard for the girl; her mother was one of the coven's stars but Ria had struggled so much. No matter how hard she studied, she didn't have Meredith's power and she would always be a mid-level witch.

I was hurt that she'd seen fit to plant a bomb under my bed. I'd thought that our relationship was okay, but evidently it wasn't. She must have harboured some sort of resentment towards me. Had I done something wrong as her coven mother that she'd gone down this dark path? Then I thought of what she'd done to Fehu and my blood boiled. Empathy aside, what she had done was *wrong*. 'Can you call Fehu?' I asked Bastion tightly.

Bastion's eyes flashed gold for a moment. 'He'll be with us shortly.'

I blinked. 'That's not possible. He must be miles away. We were in *Scotland*.'

'As I said, he's a strong flier.'

'That's not strong, that's something else. That's magic.'

'That, too.'

'He can teleport?' I asked incredulously.

'No, not exactly, but one beat of his wings can carry him a long distance.'

So Fehu was virtually supersonic. 'That's insane.'

'That's magic.' He threw back my own words. He had a valid point. 'And he's already here,' Bastion confirmed.

We left the lab through my office. Fehu was hovering outside my balcony door. When I opened it, he flew in. 'Well,' I greeted him, 'aren't you a clever bird?' He gave a happy *kraa*, landed on my shoulder and gave me an affectionate cuddle, nestling into my hair. I went to my fridge to give him some of his favourite ham. Once he'd swallowed several pieces, it was time to show him the picture.

'Do you recognise this person?' I asked, showing him the picture of Ria. Fehu tilted his head, carefully considering before letting out a negative *kraa*.

Bastion's eyes glowed again for a moment. 'He didn't see his attacker,' he said finally. 'The witch was wearing a cloak with a cowl pulled up to magically cast shadows on their face.'

Fehu was trembling slightly at the reminder of the witch who'd snapped his wings. I stroked his tummy. 'It's okay, Fehu. You're safe now,' I promised. He nuzzled me again, this time for his own benefit. After giving me one last affectionate nip on the ear, he flew to Bastion and settled on his shoulder.

Bastion's eyes glowed as the two of them conversed somehow. Because Bastion can coax, he can sense people's feelings and intentions in a way that transcends language. I guessed that skill extended to his familiar. I watched as he comforted his avian friend, settled his ruffled feathers and let him snuggle in close.

'We need to confront Ria before she does any more damage. You stay here, Fehu,' I ordered.

'*Kraa*!' he argued and hopped up and down. He shook his feathered head firmly once.

'He's coming.' Bastion's tone brooked no argument. 'He needs to see this.'

I nodded, Bastion knew his familiar best and if Fehu needed to see justice who was I to deny him? I took my athame from my bedside table and slid it into a holster that fastened on my hips. I had a potion bomb and a blade, but I doubted that I'd use either of them. Because I didn't know what to expect, I loaded my black tote full of potions and paintbrushes and put it over my shoulder.

When young Freddie had said that a girl had taken him, I'd assumed he just meant a female but now I knew it was a young girl. It was Ria. This was an absolute mess. She was so young, a misguided child but a child, nonetheless. She couldn't be trialled and treated as an adult, not yet.

She had made bad choices but she was only just starting her dark journey. Surely we could reverse the damage that had been done? I still held onto a faint hope that she'd been compelled by a wizard or something like that. After all, a compulsion could be broken.

Chapter 40

Meredith's smile was tight when she opened her door. 'Can we come in?' I asked.

'Now's not a good time. With Cindy and everything...' Her eyes darted back into the room.

'Please,' I said a little more firmly. A suspicion was growing in my mind. 'You know why we're here?'

Her shoulders sagged. 'I *knew* it wasn't Himalayan and I told her not to go and get it. Please – she's so young! She doesn't know what she's done. She's terrified.'

'Let us in and we'll talk,' I said authoritatively

Meredith held the door wide and Bastion, Fehu and I went into her home. Ria was sitting in the living room looking miserable. She was sitting on a chair, her arms wrapped around her legs, heartbreakingly young in her long flowery dress. My heart ached. She looked up as we entered, her eyes dull and resigned.

'You know why we're here,' I said softly. She nodded but said nothing. 'You've been practising black magic.' I kept my tone even. She nodded again. 'You broke Fehu's wings.' I gestured to the avian sitting on Bastion's shoulder.

Meredith flinched visibly as her daughter nodded. Her shaking hand covered her mouth as she looked at her daughter in barely disguised horror.

'You stole the hydration potions from the stores and you've been practising bloodletting,' I continued the list of accusations. 'On yourself or on others?'

'Myself,' she mumbled. 'Just me. Fehu was my first try at doing something...' She broke off. 'It was awful. I hated it. In panic I took him up to the roof and flung him off it. I thought he'd fly away but he...' she started sobbing '...he plummeted.' Straight onto my balcony.

'I thought he'd died,' she continued. She looked at Fehu. 'I'm so sorry. I'm so glad you didn't die.' He didn't respond, just leaned closer into Bastion's neck.

'You killed Cindy,' I said unable to keep the disbelief, horror and judgment out of my voice.

'No!' her mum interjected. 'That wasn't her! After the business with the bird, she told me everything. I told her to reach out to the black witch who was guiding her and tell her that she wanted out. Cindy was the price,' she said grimly.

'You can't leave,' Ria said dully. 'They won't let you.' She started to rock back and forth in the chair.

'And the bomb?' I asked softly.

Ria's head shot up. 'That wasn't me! I swear it.'

'Who then?' Bastion growled.

She shook her head miserably. 'I don't know. I don't know the names of anyone else. I'm just a black acolyte, a nobody. I don't even know the name of the witch who was instructing me. It was all done by videos, emails and online webinars.'

Great, you could now become a black witch via a computer course. Evil in the modern age.

Ria stopped rocking and her hand disappeared into her dress pocket. I tensed a little. If she'd got her hands on a potion bomb... 'I'm sorry, Mummy,' she said pitifully. 'I'm so sorry about Cindy.' She was looking at her mum.

'I know, love. It's okay.' Meredith's voice broke. 'It's going to be okay.'

'No, it's not,' Ria sobbed. 'The black coven is going to kill me.' She looked at me. 'They're everywhere, you know? Scattered in all of the covens up and down the country. I learned that much because my mentor boasted about it. All witches need to belong to a coven, so although they may be living in the Liverpool coven they're really part of the black coven. They're even on the council. They're going to kill me,' she repeated. 'But at least this way it's on my own terms.'

She pulled out a vial. She'd already removed the lid, and she downed the black potion in one. 'No!' her mother screamed, leaping forward. 'Ria! What have you taken? Tell me what you've taken!'

Bastion was there instantly. He pried her mouth open and shoved two fingers down her throat, making her gag. The black liquid gushed out – but it had already done its work. I recognised the stench of the deadly potion. It was fatal. Always.

I didn't care. I was NOT letting her die.

'Fuck!' I swore and threw my tote onto the floor. 'Wash your hands!' I barked at Bastion.

I pulled Ria to the floor and used my athame to cut open her dress so I had plenty of skin to work with. Her body was already convulsing as I opened my stasis potion and, for the second time that day, painted on *isa*, *algiz* and *sowilo*. The runes would battle the poison that she'd swallowed but it would take more than one runing to keep her alive.

I painted those same runes over and over again. I was dimly aware of Bastion comforting a sobbing Meredith whilst I painted until my hand cramped. I turned Ria over and continued to paint in mindless obsession. I would not let her die. I had lost Jake, and I couldn't bear the thought of Ria killing herself, her young life being snuffed out when it had barely started.

I was battling my own despair. I had recognised the deadly black *mordis* potion by its sight and stench and I knew it was invariably fatal, but I was an excellent potion maker; just because I hadn't saved her yet didn't mean it couldn't be done. As long as Ria lived, there was hope. So I painted until my hand was in agony and her body was covered from head to toe in runes.

The convulsions stopped and her breathing had evened. She was alive – but for how long?

I contacted Janice, my secretary at the clinic. She had all sorts of contacts and she pulled strings for us so we could have Ria admitted into a specialist facility that cared for people in comas – under a false name, of course. She would be kept alive by fluids and pumps and oxygen tanks, and her body would be forced to continue whilst I sought an antidote. I didn't even entertain the thought of failure. Mum had taught me that I could do *anything* if I worked hard enough, and Ria had just become my number-one priority.

When she was safely ensconced in the facility, I completed the paperwork for a leave of absence for her and Meredith until further notice, address to be confirmed. I signed off on it and saved it to my desktop. Technically I was supposed to send it to the coven council for filing centrally, but I had at least a week's grace before I'd be breaching the rules. I put a reminder on my phone for seven days. I was working against the clock because the moment I filed that document the black witches would know that Ria had ducked out of their organisation – and that she was still alive.

I toyed with the idea of faking her death like I had with Jake, but that hadn't worked out so well. Jake had lived his meagre life hidden and in fear of discovery. He never left the house that we'd rented; he'd been alive but it had been no life at all. I couldn't condemn Ria to the same fate. I had learned from my mistake; hard as it was to admit that I'd made a mistake with Jake, it *had* been a mistake. I recognised that now. He had been alone, isolated for so much of his life. I'd learned about the Other circus too late, and anyway it hadn't been an option for him because of his blindness.

No matter how I dressed it up, it was my fault that Jake was dead; Bastion might have been the instrument but I'd been the one wielding it. I wouldn't let the same thing happen to Ria. I was going to make a potion for her and I was going to weed out the black coven, one witch at a time if necessary.

I was declaring war on the black coven; they just didn't know it yet.

Chapter 41

Conscious of the vial in my pocket, I tried to relax. 'She'll see you now,' Melva's receptionist said, her voice tight with disapproval.

The High Priestess seer had a busy diary and I'd just leapfrogged the whole queue. I didn't care about her disapproval; yesterday had been horrific and seeing Ria intubated had shaken me. This morning I had looked myself in the eye and told myself that today I would finish the ORAL potion.

Melva owed me, like most people did. I'd worked my butt off for years helping others and now it was time to call in some debts – specifically Melva's. I didn't want to wait three weeks until a slot became available to see her, so she was fitting me in during her lunch break.

I walked into her office. Melva's purple skin was lined with age and her grey hair loosely framed her face. She was dressed in a deep-green smock, despite the old adage that purple and green should never be seen. She followed her own rules. Deep laughter lines surrounded her eyes, suggesting she smiled and laughed often though I had no idea how when she had the responsibility of being the High Priestess for all the seers. I struggled sometimes being a Coven Mother of *one* coven.

'Delegation,' Melva said as I walked in. 'Delegation is key.'

I glared. 'Stop it.'

Her smile widened. 'It is my honour to see you this day, Amber DeLea, The Huntress.'

I frowned at the title she'd gifted me at my birth. 'Yes, thank you for that one. You and I both know the only thing I've ever hunted so far is the finest Champagne.'

She flicked her eyes to Bastion. 'Protector,' she greeted him.

'High Priestess,' he responded, inclining his head respectfully.

Melva leaned forward eagerly. 'The Goddess told me that today would be a great day and my skin is tingling, Amber. What have you brought me?'

'A potion.'

'What sort of potion?' Her eagerness was endearing; she was nearly as excited as I was.

'The Other Realm Additional Length potion.'

She blinked. 'ORAL?'

I sighed. 'Yes.'

'How unfortunately named,' she commented and a smile tugged at her lips. Then she snickered and I sighed again. Even Bastion was grinning. I was never going to live this down.

'Show me your potion,' she ordered.

When I passed it to her, she took it reverently. The lavender-coloured liquid swirled in the tube; even when the vial was still, it shimmered with a pearlescent glow. It looked like magic. I loved everything about my potion – except perhaps it's unfortunate name.

Melva unstoppered the vial and sniffed at it. 'Wonderful. It smells heavenly. Hopefully it will be pleasant to imbibe.' She pulled out a crystal ball, a test-tube holder and a small bone tray. She poured a little of the potion onto the bone tray before stoppering the vial again and laying it in the test-tube holder. Then she closed her eyes and her crystal ball started to glow with a white light.

As if in a trance, Melva lifted her thumb, dipped it in the potion and smeared it across the crystal ball. Her eyes remained closed. Finally she opened them and peered into the globe. I waited breathlessly.

A triumphant look crossed her face. 'Victory, Huntress. Victory! The potion works as you intend. One vial will give you one to two weeks longer in the Other with no need for the portal. As always, it depends on your magical strength: the more magic you have, the longer the ORAL potion will boost your extension.'

Her brows drew together. 'There is a constraint, however. You cannot continue imbibing the ORAL potion indefinitely. Three or four doses in a row will work, depending on your magic, but after that you will still need the portal. After a portal recharge, you can commence imbibing the potion again and delay the use of the portal by another three to six weeks. This is wonderful news.'

She focused her eyes on me instead of the crystal ball. 'Congratulations, Amber DeLea. This is amazing.' The reverence in her tone was gratifying. 'May I?' She gestured to the vial.

I nodded, giving her permission to be the first person to test it. She downed it in one. 'Lovely,' she licked her lips. 'It even tastes good. This is going to change everything.' Her joy was infectious.

The only problem was that people are often allergic to change. My potion would be celebrated by the human half, but the elementals who ran the portals might not be so delighted – and neither would the creatures because this potion had the potential to even the playing field.

Unfortunately, not everyone wanted to play fair.

Chapter 42

'Congratulations.' Bastion's voice was warm. 'You must be thrilled.'

I was, but less so than I'd expected. Ria's condition was weighing heavily on me, and it hurt that this success, one I had dreamed of for so long, couldn't be shared with my mother. I could tell her about it, of course, but it was a coin toss whether she'd know me, let alone remember me for long enough to celebrate my victory. Still, I managed a smile. 'Thank you.'

'What do you plan to do now?' Bastion enquired curiously.

'I'll have to file the seer's verdict with the council – that will automatically validate my patent – then I can decant all the potion that I've made so far. We still have enough kelpie water and vervain for another batch, but after that I will need more ingredients. I'll reach out to Tobias for the vervain and I think Peter will be willing to provide us more – for a price.'

'And the kelpie water?'

'I have a plan,' I said vaguely as I slid into the car.

Oscar looked up as I took my seat. 'Well?' he asked impatiently.

I grinned. 'It works!'

'Ah! Congratulations, my girl! Your mum will be thrilled. I'm so proud of you.'

'Thanks, Oscar.' I leaned forward to give him an awkward hug and he kissed my forehead.

When we pulled apart he was still grinning. 'Where shall we go to celebrate?'

I laughed. 'Just home. I have some Champagne in the fridge, we can pop that.' It wasn't the finest vintage but it would do at a pinch.

'Home it is.' As Oscar started the car and we rolled forward, I pulled out my phone and rang Lucy.

'Amber!' Her voice was warm. 'How are you?'

'I'm good. I have a favour to ask.'

She laughed. 'Now I understand how annoying it is when I ring you and say I need a favour! How *are* you? It's been too long.'

'It's only been a few weeks.'

'Weeks, plural!' she said dramatically. 'See? That's ages! We used to talk every day.'

Her warmth and enthusiasm made me smile. I like Lucy. We'd recently worked together on a joint project to create a charm for Jinx and we had spoken daily. I suddenly realised how much I'd missed her infectious energy.

'Our phone bills cost me an arm and a leg!' Lucy joked. 'No,' she muttered to her wolf, Esme. 'It didn't *really* cost us an arm and a leg – we still have all of our limbs.' There was a pause. 'Obviously I wouldn't barter away our limbs without discussing it with you first. It's just a saying. It's tradition.'

'Hi, Esme,' I said to the wolf who shares Lucy's skin; their brains, however, are very different.

'She says hi, and she hopes you've had happy hunting. I think she's asking how life is, but sometimes it's hard to tell.'

'Things are good,' I assured them both.

'And how is the yummy-scrummy Bas-ti-on?' Lucy said his name in a sing-song voice.

I rolled my eyes even though she couldn't see. 'Fine.'

'Is he guarding your body?' Lucy asked, her innuendo clear.

I felt myself blush as I recalled waking up sprawled across his body again this morning. 'He's saved my life a number of times,' I said instead.

'Has he?' All joviality fled from her voice. 'Who needs their ass kicking?' There was a pause. '*You* rip off their heads, and I'll kick their asses.' There was a pause. 'Yeah, okay. I guess it makes sense for the ass-kicking to go first.'

Talking with Lucy always involved imagining Esme's contribution to the conversation. I like Esme; she is a tough broad – for a wolf – and I respect the heck out of that. 'We're working on identifying the mastermind,' I admitted. 'A black witch, certainly.'

'Another one?' Lucy asked, her tone full of horror. She'd had some fairly horrific experiences with her own black witch.

'Maybe even a couple,' I confessed.

'Fuck on a stick,' Lucy swore.

'I don't think that would be terribly comfortable,' I responded drily.

She snorted with laughter before calming down again. 'Do you need help?' The offer warmed me.

'Not with this, not yet, but I need help with something else.'

'Anything.'

I smiled again and suddenly my heart felt like it might burst. This must be what true friendship felt like. I blinked away the sudden hotness in my eyes and cleared my throat. 'Thanks. I created a potion, the Other Realm Additional Length potion. The imbiber gets to stay in the Other realm for a whole week or two per vial they drink, up to a maximum of three or four vials, depending on their magical strength.'

'Amber! This is amazing! Oh my God, I *hate* being in the Common. I'll put in an order right away. How much can I get?'

'It's still being approved by the council then you'll be able to order through the normal channels. But there's a fly in the ointment.'

'Of course there is,' Lucy sighed. 'Not an *actual* fly,' she muttered to Esme. 'Killing flies isn't the solution.'

'One of the ingredients isn't very easy to get,' I continued, ignoring Esme's fly-related input.

'What is it?'

'Water that's currently possessed by a kelpie spirit. I want your help with that.'

'You want me to what?' she asked, confused.

'I'd like you to use your piping abilities to talk to a kelpie.' I made my request as if it were a normal thing to ask of a friend, like, 'Can you pick up some wine and pipe a kelpie on the way home? Thanks.'

There was a pause. 'I thought kelpies weren't real?'

'They're very real, they're just not very well known.' Mostly because they killed everyone they encountered.

'According to the tales, I thought they were just ... malevolent water.'

'They are, if you're just malevolent blood.' I rolled my eyes. 'They're sentient, Lucy, like you and me. This potion is only sustainable if you can get them to agree to help us.'

'Why would they do that?'

'That's what we need to figure out.'

'Where do I need to go to find these kelpies?' she asked finally.

'There are a few around. There's a pair near Falkirk, near the metalwork kelpie statues, and there's a pair on Llanddwyn Island.'

'Where the hell is that?'

'In Wales, near Caernarfon.'

'Okay, nearer than Scotland,' she muttered. 'Are there none down south? I could use a holiday. Any in Dorset?'

'Is all this queen stuff getting a bit much?'

'Like you wouldn't believe.' I could almost *hear* her eyeroll.

'I don't know about Dorset. The kelpies tend to stay in one location. You could try and find another pair, I suppose – just look for an area by the river or the sea that's had a lot of deaths.'

'A *lot* of deaths?'

'Yep.'

'And you want me to go and ask the kelpies nicely?' she asked dubiously.

'Nothing easy is worth doing,' I said lightly. 'I believe in you. And if you sing nicely, they don't attack you right away.'

'Top tip.'

'Can you sing?'

'Like a nightingale,' she answered with no false modesty.

'Great. Take Manners with you.'

'You bet I'm taking his fine ass with me. I need backup.' Her voice turned sly. 'And if I help you get a sustainable ingredient stream, the coven council will give the British werewolves the potion for free.'

It was my turn to snort. 'Nice try, Lucy. I'll ensure you get a discount – a sizeable one.'

'How sizeable are we talking? I'm not risking life and limb for ten percent.'

'Fifty percent,' I offered. I'd never offered a discount that high in my life, but she was my friend after all.

'Deal,' she said briskly.

'Done and done. So mote it be.'

'So mote it be,' she agreed. 'Now that the serious stuff is out of the way, can we talk about why you've made an ORAL potion? Does Bastion not know how to—'

I hung up, blushing. Damn that sassy werewolf. Bastion raised an eyebrow at my flushed skin. 'She made a cunnilingus joke,' I sniffed. His lips twitched. 'About you,' I elaborated, keen to wipe the amused smirk off his face. 'She implied you didn't know how to...'

He scowled. 'Lucy Barrett has always been a cheeky little thing. I'll drop by when I've got some free time and teach her some respect.'

Now it was my turn to snicker.

Chapter 43

Oscar popped the cork, letting it hit the ceiling as he poured me a glass of Champagne. He gave a glass to Bastion too. 'To Amber's success,' he toasted.

'To Amber,' Bastion murmured, raising his glass.

'To success.' I took a sip and let the bubbles explode on my tongue. Oh, yum! This definitely wasn't the cheap Dom Pérignon I'd had in my fridge. I turned the bottle around so I could see the label. It was a 1907 Charles Heidsieck Champagne and far superior to any other bottle I'd tried. I gave a happy hum.

We talked quietly for a while and then I surreptitiously Googled the vintage. My eyes popped a little as I discovered it retailed for over £500 a bottle. I'd thought that Oscar had swapped the bottle, but now I turned my eyes to Bastion. He met them with his warm, dark gaze and smiled. He looked almost proud of me and it made my tummy flutter. *It's the alcohol*, I told myself firmly. *Nothing more, nothing less.*

As the hour wore on, Oscar excused himself. He kissed me on the forehead as he left. 'Congratulations again, Amber,' he murmured. 'I'm so proud, though I've no right to be.'

'You have every right to be!' The alcohol had loosened my tongue. 'You're my father in every sense of the word. You helped raise me even when my own dad abandoned me.' Did I imagine a little flinch as I said that?

He smiled. 'You're my daughter in every sense of the word,' he whispered, kissing my hair. 'Your mum would be so proud.' Past tense, because in the present she probably wouldn't grasp what a success this was. I nodded, my throat full and aching.

Oscar gave me one last hug and left me alone with Bastion, a man I had once thought was my enemy. Now I had no clue what he was. 'Are we friends?' I asked abruptly.

He studied me. 'I don't know,' he said finally. 'I don't have any of those.'

'You have Jinx.'

'She is more like family to me.'

'And I'm not like family to you?'

His eyes darkened. 'No. You're nothing like family.'

Oh. I felt a little sting of hurt and looked down at my feet.

'Friends,' he continued, moving closer. 'We could do that.' He reached out and gently tilted my chin upwards, making my eyes meet his. 'Would you like to be my friend, Amber?' The way he said my name made me shudder deliciously; I didn't think there was anything *friendly* about it.

It was just the Champagne. Too much Champagne. I swallowed and stared into his dark eyes. They warmed and I watched as they shifted from black to gold. I nodded. 'I'd like that,' I said finally.

'Friends, then.'

'Friends.'

He smiled at me and I felt like I'd climbed a mountain. I'd made a life-changing potion and I'd found a black witch in my coven, but securing Bastion's friendship was a greater achievement. It was the one thing that had made me feel like I was starting to learn the true meaning of success.

Success isn't some fancy yardstick – money, beauty, fame – it is happiness. A true friend accepts who you are and helps you become who you're meant to be. I was just starting to realise that who I was meant to be was different from everything I'd ever dreamed of. What I wanted was to be happy. And a small part of me knew Bastion would be integral in that. Friendship is important, after all.

There were more black witches out there – a whole damned coven of them, apparently – and there was Ria to save. Not to mention a position on the council that had my name on it. But all of that felt more possible with Bastion by my side.

And I was *not* going to examine why.

If you've enjoyed *Hex of the Witch,* why not have a ride along with our favourite griffin assassin in in this FREE bonus scene – written from Bastion's point of view! It's funny how much Amber misses... Grab the free scene here: https://dl.bookfunnel.com/1iisvjzelp

What's Next?

I hope you've enjoyed *Hex of the Witch!* Next up in the series is Coven of the Witch coming 27th October 2023! Someone keeps trying to kill Amber, luckily she has a live-in protector by her side. But when others are targeted too, Amber is going to face a difficult choice.

Hit the link to pre-order *Coven of the Witch* so you don't go forgetting all about little old me. In the meantime, if you'd like FREE BOOKS then join my newsletter and you can get a couple of free stories, as well as pictures of my dog and other helpful things.

Did you catch the prequel novella to this series, Rune of the Witch? It's not essential reading for the Other Witch series but I do definitely recommend it for maximal enjoyment.

Patreon

I have started my very own Patreon page! Hurrah! What is Patreon? It's a subscription service that allows you to support me AND read my books way before anyone else! For a small monthly fee you could be reading my next book, on a weekly chapter-by-chapter basis (in its roughest draft form!) in the next week or two. If you hit "Join the community" you can follow me along for free, though you won't get access to all the good stuff, like early release books, polls, live Q&A's, character art and more! You can even have a video call with me or have a character named after you! My current patrons are getting to read a novella called House Bound which isn't available anywhere else, not even to my newsletter subscribers!

If you're too impatient to wait until my next release, then Patreon is made for you! Join my patrons here.

Stay in Touch

I have been working hard on a bunch of cool things, including a new and shiny website which you'll love. Check it out at www.heathergharris.com.

If you want to hear about all my latest releases – subscribe to my newsletter for news, fun and freebies. Subscribe at my website www.heathergharris.com/subscribe.

Other Titles by Heather

Heather G. Harris' Other works:-

The Other Realm

Book 0.5 Glimmer of Dragons (a prequel story),
   Book 1 Glimmer of The Other,
   Book 2 Glimmer of Hope,
   Book 2.5 Glimmer of Christmas (a Christmas tale),
   Book 3 Glimmer of Death,
   Book 4vGlimmer of Deception,
   Book 5 Challenge of the Court,
   Book 6 Betrayal of the Court; and
   Book 7 Revival of the Court.

The Other Wolf

Book 0.5 Defender of The Pack(a prequel story),
  Book 1 Protection of the Pack,
  Book 2 Guardians of the Pack; and
  Book 3 Saviour of The Pack.

The Other Witch

Book 0.5 Rune of the Witch(a prequel story),
  Book 1 Hex of the Witch,
  Book 2 Coven of the Witch;,
  Book 3 Familiar of the Witch, and
  Book 4 Destiny of the Witch.

Heather G Harris' books co-written with Jilleen Dolbeare:-

The Portlock Paranormal Detective Series

Book 0.5 The Vampire and the case of her Dastardly Death,

Book 1 The Vampire and the case of the Wayward Werewolf,(coming March 2024)

About Heather

Heather is an urban fantasy writer and mum. She was born and raised near Windsor, which gave her the misguided impression that she was close to royalty in some way. She is not, though she once got a letter from Queen Elizabeth II's lady-in-waiting.

Heather went to university in Liverpool, where she took up skydiving and met her future husband. When she's not running around after her children, she's plotting her next book and daydreaming about vampires, dragons and kick-ass heroines.

Heather is a book lover who grew up reading Brian Jacques and Anne McCaffrey. She loves to travel and once spent a month in Thailand. She vows to return.

Want to learn more about Heather? Subscribe to her newsletter for behind-the-scenes scoops, free bonus material and a cheeky peek into her world. Her subscribers will always get the heads up about the best deals on her books.

Subscribe to her newsletter at her website www.heathergharris.com/subscribe.

Too impatient to wait for September for Heather's next book? Join her (very small!) army of supportive patrons over at Patreon.

Contact Info: www.heathergharris.com

Email: HeatherGHarrisAuthor@gmail.com

Reviews

Reviews feed Heather's soul. She'd really appreciate it if you could take a few moments to review her books on Amazon, Bookbub, or Goodreads.

Runes

No runes were harmed in the making of this book.

Heather has respectfully taken inspiration from the oldest rune system known in Europe, the *Elder Futhark* system.

As this is fiction, Heather has utilised a sprinkle of artistic license and created a few runes of her own. No offence is intended by these amendments, and they are deliberate and not errors on her part. If you'd like to see more about the Runes, there's a full post about it on Heather's Patreon page.

Made in the USA
Coppell, TX
30 December 2023

27035925R00194